THE CLARET MURDERS

A Mark Rollins Adventure

ISBN-10: 0-9856673-0-3
ISBN-13: 978-0-9856673-0-6
Library of Congress Control Number: 2012940306
Published by I-65 North, Inc.

Visit markrollinsadventures.com.
Cover Design by Tom Trebing.

Also by M. Thomas (Tom) Collins

Mark Rollins' New Career & the Women's Health Club
Mark Rollins and the Rainmaker
Mark Rollins and the Puppeteer
Marion Collins Remembers Old
Sayings and Lessons for Life
My Journey—Alice Elsie Welch Collins

THE CLARET MURDERS

A Mark Rollins Adventure

by

TOM COLLINS

Acknowledgement

The Mark Rollins series was inspired by my daughter's stories as an aerobics instructor in one of Nashville's upscale communities, while the idea for The Claret Murders *sprang from my son's Christmas gift to me in 2010—a rare bottle of Cheval Blanc.*

Men are like wine—
some turn to vinegar,
but the best improve with age.
—Pope John XXIII

PROLOGUE

Who am I?

My name is Mark Rollins. I am a senior citizen. My driver's license lists my height as five feet nine inches, my eyes as blue, and my hair as brown. I'm a cancer survivor with a military-style buzz cut—a concession to chemo—which I continue to keep. I work out regularly in an effort to stay younger than my years. Years ago I gave up fads for style. Then with the growing trend to casual attire, I eventually adopted my trademark uniform—khaki trousers, black cotton polo, and Cole Haan driving shoes. I drink martinis, straight up with an olive, and prefer Skyy or Belvedere vodka. I am also in the fortunate position of having access to people in high places and of being rather wealthy. In fact, money just keeps rolling in. What I don't spend or invest in pet projects, I turn over to the wealth management team at Goldman Sachs where it becomes little more than numbers on a computer screen.

My personal wealth came from the business side of my life. I worked as a CPA but left the profession after my investments during the early years of the computer industry paid off in a big way. In 1986 I founded Themis Legal Software. Within twenty years a third of US law firms were using Themis software, and I was considered an expert on how to run a profitable modern law firm. I published articles, made presentations, and hosted an award-winning blog. In 2007 I sold Themis to a large international corporation and retired—at least, I *intended* to retire. It didn't quite work out that way.

My access to influential people and a penchant for adventure began in the early 1990s when the US government asked me to help fledgling technology enterprises in Eastern Europe. Our government had decided it was in our national interest to encourage emerging technology in that part of the world. Unfortunately, governments outside the West feared technology—especially the Internet—in private hands. Start-up businesses were also at risk from infiltration by criminal gangs. (More than once, my wife, Sarah, and I became the targets of villainous people.) It took more than my know-how and courageous Eastern European entrepreneurs to advance global technology in that part of the world. It also required access to powerful US government forces to crush those who would prevent or preempt its advance.

My retirement plans were derailed when, for inexplicable reasons, I became the owner of the Women's Health Club located in the Brentwood suburb of Nashville, Tennessee. The WH Club, as most people call it, is an elite ladies-only facility for the socially prominent and wealthy. The members work hard to maintain youthful, seductive figures. But there is more to the club than its glitterati clientele. The club provides cover for a highly profitable, clandestine high-tech operation—useful to any number of government agencies because of its ability to operate beyond congressional oversight. Let's just say, we are not limited by the same rules, but we never seriously break the law.

CHAPTER 1

Howard J. Taylor, the Old Man

It was 10:00 a.m. Christmas Day, 1959. The sun was shining brightly and it was 55 degrees—unusually warm for that time of year. The sun made it seem even warmer.

Hidden by a dense hedge of yews, a masonry wall guarded the gray stone mansion two hundred yards off Hillsboro Road. A stone drive curved gracefully from the road to the house. Its loose brown gravel added a casual country estate feeling. It would have been inviting except for the heavy wrought iron gate—a gate that both protected and imprisoned the old man inside.

Sitting in a wheelchair, Howard J. Taylor peered through the glass French doors that opened onto the second-floor front veranda. Seventy-two years had not treated him kindly. Beaten down by a series of small strokes and laboring for every breath due to degenerative heart disease, he was more like a man of ninety. He dressed the same every morning, now with the help of his attendant, William

Walker, who the old man called his "black man." Taylor wore the uniform of a Southern gentleman banker of his generation—gray suit and vest. He wore Adler Cap-Toe shoes, their fine black leather polished to a mirror-like finish. His tie was Mogador silk—classic British stripe, navy blue and burgundy red with a fine yellow line between the wider stripes. Prepared for the walk around the garden he could no longer make, he wore a round flat-topped straw hat. His folded hands rested on the silver handle of an alabaster cane set between his legs, ready if he should try to free himself from the wheelchair. He sat and stared like a sentinel—waiting for visitors or ready to repel them. The truth is, his motive was a little of both.

Howard Taylor had been a lawyer, a banker, and the owner of an investment firm. He had money when the Depression hit and used it to buy stocks and land as prices plummeted. He took no prisoners. He made his money off the pain and sorrow of others. Some fought back—hired lawyers and sued Taylor to recover foreclosed property or for investments that went bad. He slowly acquired an intense hatred for lawyers. In Taylor's words: "Lawyers are a bunch of crooks and liars."

In the very middle of the Depression, he built the mansion that later became his lonely prison. Then World War II came. He was too old for the draft. The war ended. The economy boomed and so did his wealth. His wife had loved him. She had looked past his three indiscretions during their forty years together. The marriage produced four children he hardly knew.

There was a love child or what might more appropriately be called an "inconvenient consequence" of a night of heavy drinking and a quickie with a bosomy young black girl in his employment. He had chanced upon her that night and she had served his purposes. He provided financially through the child's college years but would have nothing else to do with her. As for the mother, she remained on his domestic staff, but he never showed the slightest bit of interest in her—he never had any.

Howard Taylor's legitimate children went their separate ways and were too busy to return home even during their mother's brief illness preceding her death in 1957. After his wife's death, he heard from the children but only when they wanted money. With their mother no longer available, they had to ask him directly. He turned them away—the way they had turned their backs on his dying wife, on their own mother.

While he was an active part of the Nashville business community, he thought he was an important man—even a great man. There were the yes-men and yes-women on his payroll, who smiled and said good morning, laughed at his infrequent jokes, and were quick to praise his wisdom and successes. There were his business peers for whom he had held the purse strings to the funds they needed to run their businesses. Then things changed.

His local investment firm was the first to be acquired. His Nashville bank merged with a large national chain a year later. Within a year, the new owners forced the old man out of both companies he had started from nothing and built into financial successes. After the mergers he was even richer, but he no longer held sway over the lives of others. His former employees and business peers soon forgot him. Their allegiance shifted to the new owners.

The old man became increasingly bitter. The occasional visitors at the gate, usually members of the church he no longer attended, were rebuffed and sent away. He refused the infrequent telephone calls from his ungrateful children so they soon stopped calling. Aside from reluctant contact with the man who managed his financial affairs and his growing dependence on William Walker and William's wife, Mildred, the old man had cut himself off from human connection.

The Walkers, in their early forties, and the younger cook lived in the caretaker's bunkhouse. It was the Walkers who dealt with the outside world when it came to the house and grounds. They managed the landscapers, repairmen, butcher, and grocer. They protected Taylor from mingling with the masses for the necessities of everyday life. Any kindness within Howard J. Taylor was reserved for William and Mildred. He had none for the other domestics. He made no allowances for their personal needs nor for holidays, including Christmas. On this Christmas Eve, he had been particularly vile to his cook. The poor woman had found the courage to speak directly to him—to beg him for a little time off on Christmas Day to be with the child in her sister's care—*her* child from *his* seed!

How could I have let that monster have me that night? she asked herself over and over. The encounter had left her feeling dirty. But she knew the answer. She had been only sixteen and he was her master. There was nothing else she could have done. But times had changed. She wasn't sixteen anymore. She was no longer afraid. She loved her child, but as for the monster who fathered it—she was filled with hate.

— ƒ —

Robert Callaway, the man who handled Taylor's financial affairs, was almost as old as Taylor himself. Callaway had worked for Taylor at the investment firm before Taylor sold it. When the new owners forced him out, Taylor hired Callaway to handle his financial affairs. Callaway was honest and unflinchingly loyal. Taylor made sure Callaway was well taken care of financially. Callaway became wealthy in his own right just by mirroring, albeit on a much smaller level, Taylor's investments. It was Callaway who dealt with the hated lawyers and despised accountants. Callaway was the only visitor admitted to the mansion—and that occurred only when the old man's signature was required.

Year after year, Callaway pushed the old man to have a will prepared. Year after year, motivated by his loathing of lawyers and bitterness toward his ungrateful children, Taylor refused. Finally, irritated by Callaway's persistence, he took pen in hand. As Callaway watched, Taylor wrote a few sentences. Then he signed, dated, and presented Callaway the paper, which read as follows:

Being of sound mind and body I write this, my first, last, and only will:

The house I live in and its grounds, including all outbuildings, furnishings, equipment, and personal property of every kind located in my house and on said grounds, shall be retained intact for the benefit of William and

Mildred Walker as long as either shall live and continue to occupy the caretaker's cottage. The executor of my will shall provide for the preservation of said property and provide William and/or Mildred Walker with an income adequate for each to live in comfort and shall provide for the medical needs of each as long as they shall live. As for the rest of my affairs, I shall not aid my heirs in their lust for my wealth; I leave that to the courts and lying lawyers to sort out.

June 2, 1956
Signed: Howard J. Taylor

— ⨍ —

William came and got the old man for his lunch. Mildred had ordered the cook to prepare his favorite—homemade beef stew with well-cooked meat and vegetables soft enough for the old man's failing gums and loose teeth. Mildred smiled at him as she served the soup. She then carefully placed on the table a tall glass of buttermilk and a slice of hot cornbread just removed from an iron skillet. He dipped the cornbread— some in the soup and some in the buttermilk. As the finale to his Christmas lunch, Mildred brought in a small plate of soft French cheese.

At William's bidding, the cook retrieved a bottle of twelve-year-old claret from the butler's pantry. The wine was first opened the night before—on Christmas Eve. The old man called it his "good stuff." He reserved this wine for himself. The cook did not smile as she poured him an ample glass. Without a word, she returned to the kitchen, taking the bottle and its unpoured contents with her.

After lunch William took Taylor to his room for his routine midday nap. William always woke him at 3:00 p.m., and then the old man would resume his position as sentry. At three o'clock on this Christmas afternoon, William could not wake him—the old man was dead.

No one had come to the gate—no one to be welcomed or repelled.

Chapter 2

Henry L. Burroughs III, Attorney at Law

Henry L. Burroughs III was an asshole. But he was also "old Nashville." He belonged to the right club, the Belle Meade Country Club, and socialized with all the right people. That meant business for the law firm, so the other partners tolerated him. They responded to complaints from secretaries and associates with the quick dismissal: "That's just Henry's way. It isn't personal. You just have to remember who he is; don't let his manner upset you."

In Henry's world, people were ants—you were either a big black ant or a pissant. Henry and his kind were the big black ants. He was a law partner and a Burroughs. Who the hell did people in the office think they were? Their job was to make him look good. That was their purpose—their only purpose.

It was a cold, rainy Monday morning in early October. The traffic had been a bitch and Henry's mood was as foul as the weather as he came through the double glass doors of the law firm Chambers and White. The receptionist saw him coming and nervously attempted to smile as she greeted him, "Good morning, Mr. Burroughs."

He stopped and stared at the young girl. It was an ugly stare. It took her breath away, and she looked down at her desk. She felt exposed. She wanted to cross her arms over her breasts—to somehow hide from this awful man.

When he spoke, the veins on his forehead bulged. He shouted angrily as if he wanted the entire office to hear: "You stupid cow! Look out the damn window. Does that look like a *good* morning?" She was already choking back tears, but Burroughs wasn't through with this pissant. "You can't even do the simple-ass job of answering the phone right. I called to let my secretary know I was running late. The phone rang *five* times before you fucking answered—and *then* you had the audacity to put me on *hold*!"

"I'm sorry, Mr. Burroughs . . . The phones were so busy . . . I thought it was better to put one of us on hold rather than a client."

"One of *us*? You sad, sad little girl. What makes you think you're one of *us*? You're a puny telephone operator—and you can't even do *that* right. Don't you *ever* put me on hold *again*. You understand?"

Tears streamed down Betty Foster's face as she nodded. Lines of running mascara turned her face into that of a cartoon character.

Burroughs laughed. "You look like shit. Fix yourself before someone important comes through that door—like a client."

Burroughs walked away, heading for his office. There was a smug grin on his face. He had made someone miserable. He had exercised power over her. He liked that. It was good practice. Burroughs was a litigator.

He saw the new partner, Ann Sims, down the hall. She was breathtakingly glamorous—more Monroe than Twiggy. She knew what nature had given her, and she didn't hide it behind loose-fitting outfits or the "power" suits preferred by other women in the office. She opted for formfitting dresses or pencil skirts with tight silk blouses, and she liked red. He understood she was a moneyed person. She was accepted in Belle Meade and even into the Swan Ball circles, but that didn't mean much to Henry. He calculated that she had made those connections because of her body—slept her way into the right places. But unfortunately for her, he thought, she hadn't yet slept with the right person—him.

Burroughs took little notice of Ann during the four years that she was just another associate attorney in the law firm, but from the day she became a partner, he had started to work on her. He planned to break down her defenses, just as he did with hostile witnesses. *That is one cow I wouldn't mind bedding,* he thought as he walked down the hall toward her. *She may be a partner, but she's not in my league. She'll learn she has a choice—become part of my loyal group or suffer the consequences. I'll make her feel insecure—destroy her confidence. I'll expose every mistake she makes. Hell, I'll invent mistakes for her. She'll come to me before I'm through with her, that is, if I want her then.*

Henry knew how to intimidate people. He got in Ann's personal space and hissed, "You really think that outfit is appropriate for a partner in this law firm?"

She just looked at him and smiled.

He didn't stop. He raised his voice to make sure others would hear. "You look like a *whore*."

Ann Sims was not passive as he had imagined. She slowly, seductively licked her lips, and Henry flinched. The truth is he filled with lust. She put her hand on his bicep and let it slide down to his wrist. He began to feel aroused. Then she struck back. "Henry, I just love to see your cheery face in the mornings. I wore this outfit just to turn you on. I understand you are particularly fond of whores."

"Fuck you, Sims." He stormed down the hall, and those who saw him coming got out of the way.

"Coffee—and make it snappy," growled Burroughs as he pushed past his secretary, Judy Graves, and into his office.

Judy had heard the exchange between Burroughs and Sims and knew she was in for a verbal lashing. He would take it out on her as he always did.

While Judy went for coffee, Henry planned his next attack on Sims. The bitch would pay. He took a sheet of paper from the printer on his credenza, found an envelope with no return address, and wrote an anonymous complaint to the Tennessee Bar:

> *Gentlemen, it is with great reluctance that I must advise you of gross misconduct by a member of the Bar. Miss Ann Sims,*

an attorney with the firm of Chambers and White, attempted to seduce me in order to secure my business. Shocked by such inappropriate behavior, I made some inquires among friends in the business community and discovered that Miss Sims' behavior with me appears to be standard operating procedure for her. Several business associates reported receiving sex from her in exchange for moving their legal business to her firm.

Signed: A Concerned Citizen

Judy returned with his coffee. He was folding the hand-written note and putting it into the envelope as she placed the saucer and cup of coffee on his desk. She had taken care to prepare it just the way he liked and served it in fine china. Burroughs was no mug man.

Noticing the envelope in his hand, she asked, "Would you like me to take care of that for you, Mr. Burroughs?"

He didn't look up, but quickly demanded: "Get me a stamp!"

"A stamp? Don't you want me to have the mailroom handle that?"

"Would I ask for a stamp if I did? You *do* understand English, don't you? I. Said. Get. Me. A. Stamp. How many times do I have to tell you something?" Not really expecting her to answer, he picked up the cup of coffee. He tasted it and made a face. "What the shit is this? It is cold as hell and tastes like a fucking truckstop. Take this away! Bring me a fresh cup and don't forget the goddamn stamp."

Judy had learned to say nothing. If she said anything, it just opened her up for more insults. She took the cup and walked out of his office. He would get his fresh cup of coffee, but she was going to add something extra.

CHAPTER 3

Judy Graves, Legal Secretary

Judy Graves, an accomplished, highly-thought-of legal secretary, had come to work for Chambers and White four years ago at the age of thirty-nine. She had worked seventeen years for a small Nashville firm, Adams and Davis, with offices on Second Avenue close to the courthouse. Judy admired both men. Adams and Davis were African American and had matured during Nashville's period of racial unrest. Unfortunately, these veterans of the civil rights movement were elderly. After Adams died and Davis finally announced his retirement, Judy had no alternative but to reenter the job market.

The law firm of Chambers and White had defended several cases involving racial discrimination with Adams and Davis on the other side. Since A&D, as they were sometimes called, was a small firm and its aging partners were not always accessible, Judy was often the person opposing attorneys dealt with. The lawyers at Chambers and

White knew her work and quickly made an offer that she couldn't refuse.

Adams and Davis were men comfortable in their own skins. There were no large egos. No infighting in their firm. Neither needed large offices or fancy cars as a testament to their value. They knew their worth as did the people who turned to them for help or met them on the battlefield of justice. Judy's seventeen years at Adams and Davis had not prepared her for the raging egos and internal politics of a large firm like Chambers and White.

Judy was born into an all-woman household. For the first part of her life, the matriarch of the family was her great aunt, Wilma Graves. Wilma had raised Judy's mother, Emily. Peaches Graves was Emily's real mother—Judy's grandmother. In 1947, Peaches, a fourteen-year-old black girl, moved to the big estate on Hillsboro Road and began working in the kitchen of an "old moneyed" Nashville family. Peaches was devoted to the lady of the house, Rebecca Taylor, who patiently taught Peaches her duties and treated her mistakes gently. But Peaches grew to hate the lord of the house. Rebecca's husband, Howard J. Taylor, practiced neither patience nor gentleness. He treated his wife poorly and bullied the domestic staff. But her dislike became hatred the night he took Peaches to his secret room. She was only sixteen. She served his purposes that night and that was all. She hadn't resisted. She hadn't known how. He was Master Taylor. She was a servant.

Peaches continued to work in the big house and nine months later gave birth to Emily in her small bedroom in the bunkhouse. Judy's great-aunt, Wilma Graves, came to the big house the next day. Like the grocer or milkman, she came to the kitchen door where she took delivery of the tiny baby girl. Wilma took the newborn home and became Emily's stand-in mother.

There wasn't a lot of talk about men in the Graves's household. Wilma had never married nor had children. Emily was the product of a loveless encounter that bred in her mother a lifelong distrust and hatred for men. Judy, too, was nothing more than the consequence of an un-protected evening of college lust between her light-brown mother and the all-white quarterback of her university's football team.

By the time Judy was twelve, her mother, Emily, was an English professor at Fisk University, and as during the years she spent pursuing her education, she had little time to spend with her daughter. That's when another person came into Judy's life. Judy's great-aunt, Wilma, died from pneumonia, and Judy's grandmother, Peaches, finally left the only home she had known since age fourteen and, in 1979, moved in with her daughter and granddaughter to care for the soon-to-be teenager.

Neither Peaches nor Emily ever expressed regret about the absence of men in their lives. They distrusted men, or perhaps more accurately, they trusted men to ruin you. "They don't care nothin' about you. All they want is to sat-isfy their urges. The only thing men are good for is makin' babies. It don't make any difference if you want them or not." Peaches tutored Judy on how to survive in this world as a black girl—even a light-skinned one. Slowly Judy figured out that the money the family received monthly, the money that enabled Judy's mother, Emily, to earn her PhD, were payments from Emily's father. Peaches never spoke his name, but Judy knew it had to be Howard J. Taylor. Not only was Judy's grandfather white, he also was one of the richest men in Nashville.

Emily died of cancer at fifty-three. Peaches' heart gave out at age seventy-six, shortly after Judy joined the law firm of Chambers and White. Just before she died, she gave Judy a tiny, violet-colored bottle. It looked very old and probably was originally made to hold perfume. Peaches said, "Honey, I made what's inside this bottle myself. A black woman in this world needs protection, and this was mine. You get a man trying to do you wrong—this is a way to strike back. You have to be very careful, girl. A drop will make him too sick to care about you. More than a drop and that man won't be doing anybody wrong ever again. You understand?"

Judy had nodded, but she wasn't really sure she understood. She still carried the little bottle in her purse. It was all she had left of her grandmother, perhaps the most important person in her life.

Chapter 4

Eli Campbell, Managing Partner

Eli Campbell, managing partner of Chambers and White, walked into the break room carrying an empty mug. Partners seldom entered the room, but Eli was the exception. He practiced "management by wandering around." Chatting with the staff while pouring his own coffee or biting into a hot Krispy Kreme doughnut gave him an insight that none of the other partners had. Unlike the other partners, he was friendly, outgoing, and approachable when in the office. But, that was a practiced facade.

Many professions—including medical, accounting, and legal—often depend on the exploitation of the young. Long hours, missed vacations, and working weekends are the price those entering the profession have to pay. Making the way to the top, the ability to enjoy life increases and weighs on the backs of those who follow. Eli was just as ambitious as the other partners. He loved traveling first class, drinking nice wines, and dining in the best restaurants. His well-honed people skills were just a means to an end.

Campbell was five feet ten inches, and usually wore a brown suit, white button-down oxford shirt, traditional striped tie, and brown Johnston & Murphy wingtips. He was an ex-Marine—Special Forces. At forty-two, he still had that G.I. Joe look about him. His mild manner was never confused with weakness. People could tell this wasn't a man to be trifled with. He had been a warrior, one trained to kill. And he *had* killed—with guns, knives, and even his bare hands. A bachelor, he was handsome in a rugged way. There were whispers about him and Ann Sims. He was older, but glamour and sex appeal made them seem an ideal couple—the brute and the beauty.

Today, as he entered the break room, Eli found a teary-eyed receptionist seated at a small table in the center of the room. Judy Graves was consoling her. "Betty, don't let him get to you like this. You know how that bastard is. You are the best receptionist we've ever had. The man just hates life and takes it out on the rest of us."

Hearing someone enter, Judy looked up and saw the managing partner. "I'm sorry, Mr. Campbell, but the man is an animal. Something really needs to be done about him."

Campbell didn't have to ask who they were talking about. He had overheard the exchange between Burroughs and Sims. He knew the man was an asshole. As managing partner, he had given each member of the executive committee a copy of the *Harvard Business Review* essay by Stanford professor Robert Sutton in which Sutton spelled it out. Office bullies aren't just a nuisance, but a serious and costly threat to employee morale and business success.

To Campbell, that meant Burroughs was costing the partners money. He was putting the future of the firm at risk. Nevertheless, the executive committee lacked the courage or fortitude to do anything about Burroughs. They always pointed to the business he brought into the firm. Campbell understood that each had mentally calculated the impact on their personal income if that business went away. They, however, had not calculated the downside—the even greater cost of high staff turnover, the loss of needed talent as young associates bailed out to go elsewhere, or the impact on recruitment. Word had gotten out, and the firm was no longer able to attract the best candidates coming out of the Vanderbilt or University of Tennessee law schools.

Campbell had commanded men in battle. He had made life-and-death decisions on the spot—and carried them out quickly. Even after fifteen years as a lawyer, including five as managing partner, he still wasn't accustomed to dealing with people who couldn't or wouldn't make a decision. He found ways to get around such people—to take the actions he considered necessary. He would do that in this case as well. He just hadn't decided how . . . yet.

Judy turned her back to Campbell and walked to the coffee bar to begin preparing the new cup of coffee her boss had demanded. She was thinking of her grandmother, Peaches, who had worked all those years in the kitchen of that man she hated so completely. Peaches used to laugh and tell Judy stories about how she and other household staff got even with the "Lord of the House" as her grandmother called him. That is what Burroughs was to Judy. Here she was, a highly paid legal secretary, fetching coffee for *her* Lord of the House. She muttered under her breath, "Yes, Master Burroughs, I'll fetch your coffee for you."

She filled the cup with hot water to warm the china. She emptied it, then filled it with coffee from the insulated dispenser, added half a pack of the yellow sweetener and just a splash of half-and-half. She stirred the coffee slowly. When she saw that Campbell was busy talking to Betty, Judy added something else after she mouthed the words, "This is for you, Grandmother."

When she turned around, Campbell asked, "Is that coffee for your boss?"

"Yes. He rejected the first one I prepared—said it was cold and tasted like truckstop coffee." Judy shrugged her shoulders as she added, "He probably won't be satisfied with this one either. Mr. Campbell, I work hard for that man. I'm good at my job, but he makes me feel terrible on a daily basis. I don't think I can do this much longer."

Campbell got up and walked over to the coffee bar as he said, "Judy, give me the coffee. I'll deliver it. I think it's time that Mr. Burroughs and I come to an understanding."

Judy quickly replied, "He'll have me fired, Mr. Campbell. He'll think I went to you about him."

"You don't need to worry about that, Judy."

— ʃ —

Campbell closed the door behind him as he entered Burroughs's office. The curmudgeon was seated behind his campaign desk reading the draft of the brief his secretary had come in early that morning to transcribe.

Burroughs didn't look up until he saw the managing partner's hand placing the coffee on his desk. "What the hell? Where's my secretary?"

"Henry, it's time you and I had a little talk."

Henry Burroughs was not a healthy fifty-two-year-old man. In spite of all his bluster and bluff, he was not very strong. He was asthmatic and had lived most of his life feeling as if an elephant were sitting on his chest. His breathing was labored. His suits hid a frail, thin body. But his powerful position made him unafraid of people like Eli.

"You bet it is, Mr. Campbell. You here to take up for your little woman? Or maybe you didn't like my questioning your motives in the partners's meeting. I still want to know why you are handling the Taylor auction yourself. That's a job for a junior member of the firm, not our big important managing partner. Is there something in it for you we don't know about? I think I'll pay a visit to the estate. What do you say, old man? Want to show me around the place?"

"Henry, what makes you such a jerk?"

"Get off it, Campbell. We're all looking out for number one. Don't try to play Mr. Goody Two-Shoes with me. If you aren't already bedding Sims, you're working on it. If you haven't figured out a way for the Taylor thing to put money in your pocket, you're working on that too. Whatever it is, I'll figure it out."

When Eli Campbell left Henry Burroughs's office at 10:30 that morning, he closed the door behind him. Judy Graves was behind her desk in the small anteroom through which one had to pass for access to her boss's office. Campbell smiled slightly and said to the secretary, "Leave his door closed for a while; he has some thinking to do. And Judy, I don't think you will have to worry about him anymore."

— ✗ —

It was 3:00 p.m. and Henry Burroughs had still not come out of his office. He had not buzzed her on the intercom—had not even asked her to call out for lunch to be brought in. None of that was normal. Her boss almost never closed his door. He wanted others to hear him when he bullied associates working on his cases or when he shouted at opposing lawyers over the phone.

Judy had plenty of work to keep her busy and actually enjoyed the peace and quiet, but every hour on the hour she glanced at his closed door. She finally decided to check for herself.

She opened the door. Henry Burroughs was sitting with his head down on folded arms resting on his desk. She softly called out his name, "Mr. Burroughs?" When he didn't reply or move, Judy walked across the room to his desk. She touched him. He was cold as a stone—dead! Her heart skipped a beat and her mind began racing.

She saw the empty cup and saucer and grabbed them. She glanced around for the envelope with the handwritten address—the one for which she had gotten the stamp. She didn't know what was in the letter or to whom he was mailing it, but she knew him, so she knew that the letter would be harmful to someone. If the letter had been in his outbox, she would have taken it along with the cup, but it wasn't there.

She went back to her desk and put the empty cup and the saucer in a drawer. She would wash them and put them away later. She called 911. Then, because he was the managing partner, she went to find Campbell to tell him that she had found her boss dead at his desk.

She felt really good—the best she had felt in years.

The medical examiner's report listed cause of death as heart failure. Judy Graves didn't bother to go to the funeral. Eli Campbell and Ann Sims did.

Chapter 5

Ann Sims, Judy's New Boss

When Ann arrived the morning after the funeral, Judy was sitting in the secretary cubical across from her office. Ann had been without a secretary of her own since making partner. Until now, she had shared a secretary with the senior associate in the office next to her, Ronald Howard.

Judy rose to greet her new boss and followed Sims into her office. "Good morning, Ms. Sims. How would you like your coffee?"

"Good morning to you, Judy. I can handle my own coffee requirements. What I can't do is type 120 words a minute or (pointing to the files piled up on her desk and waving to those lining the floor along the wall behind her desk) keep these damn files straight and out of the way."

"Well, I can certainly do both of those things."

"Then we are going to be a great team, Judy."

"Wonderful! I can't tell you how happy I was this morning when they told me I was to be your legal assistant. Just for the record, I will be happy to do the coffee thing anytime you need me to."

"Thanks, Judy, I won't ask you unless I am really pressed for time. Although there may be times when we have a client visiting and need beverages or lunch taken care of for us."

"I can handle it, Ms. Sims."

"Judy, first things first. I need you to get all the files on the Taylor estate. Mr. Campbell has dumped the auction thing in my lap. For some reason, he has decided to recuse himself from it. I don't believe there is much for us to do. The auction is already scheduled for sometime in the next two weeks. We just have to make sure that all the paperwork is handled properly and on time."

"Got it, Ms. Sims, but this is kind of touchy for me."

"How so?"

"My grandmother worked in the Taylor kitchen years ago. I have never been to the mansion, but she told me a lot of stories about the place. They were not all nice. I'm afraid she didn't have very pleasant memories about her time there."

"Anything I should know?"

"I don't think so."

"Well, it's a strange situation. The place is being auctioned as is—lock, stock, and barrel. Everything goes. I understand that it is almost as if they locked the doors fifty years ago and walked away. Supposedly there are cars in the carriage house that haven't been driven since 1959. The buyer is getting a real grab bag. No one is sure about valuation. The house is a tear down, but some of the furniture and other things have value as antiques. And, of course, the land is ripe for development once we get out of this damn recession and people start buying homes again."

"My grandmother talked about a secret room, Ms. Sims. There may be things in that house no one knows about."

"Maybe I should talk to your grandmother."

"You would have to speak loudly or get out your Ouija board. She isn't with us anymore."

"Sorry to hear that. Eli—Mr. Campbell—wants me to concentrate on handling the paperwork, but I think it would be fun to have a go at the place and see if we can turn up a hidden treasure. What about it, Judy? Would you be interested in tagging along?"

"I don't think so. My grandmother's memories were pretty dark. Visiting the place would not be pleasant for me, knowing what I know. She was not treated kindly by the Lord of the House—'Master Taylor' as she used to call him."

"I understand. It was a different time."

"For blacks, yes it was. But in all honesty, there is still some changing that needs to be done. My last four years working for Mr. Burroughs were not the most pleasant of my life. I hope it wasn't because I'm an African American woman."

"No, Judy, it wasn't. Burroughs was awful to everyone. Race didn't have anything to do with it."

"I'll get started on the files. But don't forget to look for the secret room if you do go there. I remember she said that was where he kept the 'good stuff.' I was young and not always interested in her stories. I didn't ask her what she meant by 'good stuff.'" Judy started to walk away, and then looked back over her shoulder and said, "Oh, you need to watch the weather. I hope it stays nice for your auction, but this is the time of year we get some pretty strong storms—tornadoes included."

"Thanks for the reminder. Maybe we should order tents."

Ann's office phone began to ring.

"Shall I get that?" Judy asked.

"No, I'll get it. I want you working on those files."

Ann picked up the handset, "This is Ann Sims."

"Ms. Sims, you don't know me, but I'm afraid I have some bad news for you. It is about Churchill."

Chapter 6

Mark Rollins

As usual, there was an armada of construction vehicles blockading the entrance to Ann's condominium complex. The luxury condominiums on Bowling Avenue are not far from the original site of the Richland Country Club. The condos were not new, but the location commanded top dollar. Every time one of the units turned over, the new owners gutted the interior and brought the property up to date. I elected to park nearby and walk the rest of the way.

The lady who met me at the door was probably in her early to mid-thirties. I had seen her many times at the Women's Health Club; she was the kind of woman that men can't help but notice but who often lead a lonely life. It wasn't just beauty; it was glamour—an allure or sexuality that most men fear out of insecurity. She was wearing a wine-colored velour robe—a designer piece, probably from Calvin Klein's exclusive collection. Her hair and makeup suggested she was preparing for a night out—I guessed dinner and the symphony or one of Nashville's charity events.

"Thanks for coming, Mr. Rollins."

"I hope I can help, Ms. Sims."

Ann Sims had called my cell phone during a lunch celebration at Sperry's. My team and I had just wrapped up a case. A friend of mine had been murdered in Nashville's Printers Alley, and we had made the world a better place by sending his killer to hell. It was worth celebrating. (The details of this case are documented in the book *Mark Rollins and the Puppeteer*.)

"Please call me Ann."

"Then you must drop the Mr. Rollins and call me Mark."

She led me across the room to one of two floral man-size chairs that directly faced a snow-white couch where she sat down. She sat upright with excellent posture. The robe fell away revealing million-dollar legs held close together.

"Mark, I don't have long. I'm a cochair of the Swan Ball, scheduled for later this month and tonight there's a pre-event for our most important Nashville donors. Lord Deed Millhouse from London is picking me up in an hour."

"What is so important that you need to talk to me today?"

"It is my dog, Churchill. He was murdered today. I want you to track down the killer and make sure he doesn't get away with it."

I looked at her in stunned silence, trying to find words to respond. She certainly wasn't the kind of woman you don't want to please. But a *dog*—? The best I could come up with was "Your dog? I don't understand."

"Mark, I know you've helped other members of your fitness club. Well, I'm a member of the WHC, and I need your help. I'm not a girl who turns the other cheek. I'm also an attorney with the firm of Chambers and White and I believe in justice. The man who killed my Churchill has to pay for his crime."

Her stare didn't waver. Beauty and intellect—this wasn't a dumb beauty queen. I got the feeling that she was a person who always got what she wanted, and got it through determination and a willingness to do whatever it took. I was going to do her bidding, and she knew it.

"Tell me what happened."

"I don't know exactly what happened, Mark, but your brother was a witness."

"My brother? Glen?" I was dumbfounded and curious at the same time.

"Yes. He called and told me. The killer was a policeman—a Belle Meade policeman!"

I looked at her, at a loss for words.

She wiped away a tear from the corner of her eye. That tear destroyed what tiny little self-control I had left—I was helplessly under her spell.

"Please," she said, "I can't talk about it anymore, and I have to finish dressing. Will you talk to your brother?"

What else could I do? I said, "Yes, of course."

CHAPTER 7

Lord Deed Millhouse

A s I left the condo, I saw a limo navigating through the construction vehicles. The driver pulled up to the curb adjacent to the short brick walkway to the first-floor entrance of Sims's townhouse. Lord Deed Millhouse, I presumed.

For the last few days, I had been walking with a cane because of leg pain extending from the left hip to the knee—the result of a deep tissue massage gone wrong. It took a few steps walking across the grassy lawn of the complex toward my car before the pain reminded me about the walking stick I had left behind. I could have survived without it, but it gave me an excuse to check out this Lord Millhouse. I am a curious fellow.

The chauffer opened the back passenger door, and Lord Millhouse exited the limousine with practiced ease. Few men look comfortable in white tie and tails. Millhouse was one who did. He appeared to be fit and in his mid-forties. He had salt-and-pepper hair and stood about five feet eleven inches with Reagan-like posture. I guessed his weight at 180 pounds. I have seen a lot of men in formal attire, most of it rented, especially white-tie attire. Face it; most of us don't have a "monkey suit" hanging in our closets. Clearly, Lord Millhouse's outfit wasn't rented. The tailcoat was a perfect fit, as was the white waistcoat that properly covered his trouser waistline but did not extend below the front of the tailcoat. The white bow tie was done to perfection, and the shirt collar was neither tight nor loose. Just the right amount of cuff was showing and the trousers had the perfect break over his patent leather shoes. He definitely looked the part.

The Swan Ball, one of the premier charity events in the United States, was still a few weeks away, so I assumed tonight's white-tie event was a practice run. The ball itself is strictly high society—a showplace event for Nashville's rich and famous—although the guest list always includes prominent East and West Coast notables as well as a smattering of international jet-setters. The glittery event is always held on the grounds of the Cheekwood Botanical Garden and Museum of Art.

Cheekwood is the mansion that Maxwell House coffee built. Its president, Leslie Cheek, built the native limestone house and laid out the sixty acres of gardens back in the thirties. Eventually, the mansion and its palatial grounds were donated for use as an art museum and botanical garden.

The door to the condo opened just as Lord Millhouse and I awkwardly met at the bottom of Ann's front steps. The lord glanced at me with a quizzical expression—as if to say, "Who are you and what are you doing in my space?"

Ms. Sims stood in the doorway holding my cane. Full figured is not the right description because Ann was not Rubenesque. Hers was a cover girl figure—the kind artists draw for men's calendars that end up glued to locker doors. She had the curves—all of them—and all in the right places. Looking at her, neither Millhouse nor I said anything. I think we both were drinking in her full image, and words would have just gotten in the way. She was wearing a shimmering red and orange skintight gown that accentuated her curves. The dress seemed to be made entirely out of iridescent overlapping sequins shaped like fish scales. She was mermaid-like—an exotic fish. I understood for the first time the legends of seafaring men lured to their death as they were hypnotically drawn off course by beautiful but deadly women-like creatures of the sea.

The alluring creature standing in front of us held out my cane and said, "Mark, you forgot this." I took it—without saying a word.

She turned to the British nobleman. "Lord Millhouse, I would like you to meet Mr. Mark Rollins. Mr. Rollins was visiting me moments ago. He is helping me with a problem concerning my pet." Looking back at me she added, "Mark, Lord Millhouse is visiting Nashville from London and will be accompanying me this evening."

I held out my hand and Millhouse shook it as I said, "It is a pleasure to meet you, sir. I must say that you will be the envy of every man at the festivities tonight."

"The pleasure is mine, Mr. Rollins. And, my good man, you are undoubtedly correct. It will require great skill to keep her from being stolen away." He looked at Ann and said, "My dear, you do look absolutely stunning." He was one step down from where Ann stood, and from there he admiringly looked up at her, holding out his hand. She took it, and the two of them began walking toward the limousine where the driver stood holding the door. She looked back at me and mouthed the words, "Call me."

I watched them drive away—the lady and the diplomat. (I didn't actually know if he was a diplomat; the British just always seem that way.) I remember shopping in Harrods years ago with my wife, Sarah. Two male clerks in the fine china department were arguing about where to display certain items. You could just imagine that they were resolving some international dispute or negotiating the terms of a treaty. The British simply look and sound like my image of a diplomat or statesman on the world stage. They simply sound more important than the rest of us.

Lord Deed Millhouse was almost the perfect British gentleman stereotype—almost, but not exactly. In spite of everything, there was something un-English about him that made me want to do a little research on the man. We live in a time when you can buy anything over the Internet and that includes a title of nobility. For $29.99, anyone can become a lord.

What bothered me? It was his teeth. Well-educated British men have a lot going for them, but their teeth aren't usually among those things. Lord Millhouse had a perfect set of white choppers, the kind you find in Hollywood, not in London. I would have to learn more about Ann's lord.

For now, I thought, *I'm going to go home to the alluring lady of my dreams—the woman with whom I've spent nearly fifty years. She won't be wearing a skintight iridescent dress, but even in her blue jeans, she is still beautiful and commands complete power over me.*

CHAPTER 8

Paul Walton, Professor of English

It was Tuesday, and I couldn't put off calling Ms. Sims any longer. I didn't have any excuses left. On Friday, I had agreed to investigate the death of her dog. I suppose I had been procrastinating, but the truth is there wasn't much I could accomplish over the weekend anyway. As for Monday, I just couldn't tell Sarah that a dog investigation was more important than her plans to look at investment property in the country.

"Mark, I'm so glad you called; I was getting worried. Do you have anything to report about Churchill?"

"No, I haven't had a chance to talk to my brother yet. I'm going to have lunch with him today to discuss the matter. How was your event the other evening? According to the news, you have already set a fundraising record, and the big Ball is still several weeks away."

"Oh, it was lovely, but the cochair job involves a lot of work. I'm glad it's almost over. And, between you and me, Deed—Lord Millhouse—is turning out to be a real pest.

I'll be glad when he goes back to London. In fact, he's one of the reasons I was hoping you would call this morning. I need to talk to you about my man problems. It isn't just him. I seem to run into the same pattern with all the men I get involved with."

"Oh?"

"The truth is there aren't many. A lot of people assume I lead a glamorous life."

"I can understand why. You do have that movie star look about you."

"I'll take that as a compliment."

"As it was meant."

"I'm really pretty much a work-and-home person. It's not that I wouldn't like to go out more often. It's just that men seem reluctant to ask me out. My therapist says they are afraid of rejection. The problem is that the ones who do ask me out turn out to be overly possessive."

"Your Lord Millhouse is a jealous man?"

"Well, yes, but he isn't the worst. Unfortunately, I have a husband few people know about. I married him while I was still in law school, and I've been trying to get out of the marriage ever since. The divorce is supposed to be finalized in a few more days."

"I had no idea. Does he live in Nashville?"

"No, thank goodness. He's still a professor at Emory in Atlanta. Not in the law school. He's in the English de-partment—specializes in literature, British masterpieces. I was young. He was so intelligent. He swept me off my feet. What I didn't know was that he is unstable. While he was studying at Berkeley, he got into drugs and a protest movement of some kind. I don't even know what they were protesting. I don't think they knew either. They were just angry at the world and wanted to blow up things and hurt people. I learned about his violent side too late. All I had to do was smile at another man to set him off. He can be a wild man. I was naïve enough to be flattered by his possessiveness at first."

"Was he physically abusive?"

"Only once to me—but that was enough! I left him, but he wouldn't leave me alone. When I was still at Emory, he would show up unannounced at my apartment. If I went out with someone, Paul would call my date and threaten him. He called all the time begging me to come back to him. That is not something I would ever do!"

"But you've been away from Emory for some time now."

"Yes, almost five years. It's taken me that long to get a divorce. But he's started calling again—says he can't live without me, can't stand the thought of me being with another man, and all that other stuff you read about happening in an abusive relationship. He was apparently watching my place the night you visited me. He called right after you left. Said he had you in his gunsight and that it took all his strength not to pull the trigger. When I opened the door that evening holding your cane, I was actually looking for him."

"So he thought I was your lover?"

"Yes. Then Deed showed up. When I got home that night, there was a message on my phone—it was Paul. That's his name, Paul Walton. He called me a whore and every other ugly name he could think of. Apparently, he didn't care for my gown and didn't like the idea of two men on my doorstep."

"May I listen to the message?"

"No, I immediately erased it. I knew I had done the wrong thing the minute I punched the number seven on my phone. I'm a lawyer and I knew better, but I was so angry—well, I should say frightened. I know this is the most dangerous time. If Paul is capable of hurting someone, this is when it will happen. Divorce has finality to it. It legally cuts any bond between us. This is the time most abused women are killed."

"What do you want me to do?"

"I don't want to die. You're the only person I could think of to keep me safe."

"Ann, you need to go to the police."

"I will. I promise to file for a restraining order. There was one in effect in Georgia, but not here. But, Mark, if you've done any research in this area, you must know that for a woman in an abusive relationship, getting a judge to issue a restraining order can be like signing her own death warrant."

"I understand, Ann. I've read David Buss's work on evolutionary physiology, and according to him, killing is fundamental to the nature of men like Paul because in eons of human evolution, murder has been so beneficial in reproductive competition. Killing became an instinctive act—sometimes the woman who strayed was murdered; sometimes it was the interloping male. By killing the woman, the male tells other prospective partners what happens to those who reject him. By killing the male competitor, the man not only eliminates that specific competitor, he also warns off others. Your Paul is being driven by motives evolved over thousands and thousands of years. It illustrates just how close all of us live to our primitive natures."

"But Mark, we don't live in caves."

"Ann, we still have those primitive drives. Modern laws and morals keep primitive traits in check for most of us. But take away the risk of getting caught and punished, and the worst in us is unleashed. In Kosovo, neighbors turned on neighbors—men killed their 'male competitors' and raped their daughters and wives. The anomaly is now—what we think of as modern or civilized time. Reproductive killing was normal behavior for thousands of years."

"That's so frightening to think about. I suppose it means I was right to be afraid of what Paul might do. So you do agree that I need protection?"

"From Paul Walton, yes! What about Millhouse? Are you afraid of him too?"

"He's a pest, but no. I'm not really afraid of him. But with Paul hanging around, I think it would be smart for him to get out of town, so to speak."

"Where is Millhouse staying?"

"Union Station. He has a wonderful suite."

"You stayed with him?"

"Well, no, but he talked so much about the hotel and its history that I wanted to see it. So we stopped there for a nightcap. Mark, there is one other thing I should tell you. There is someone at the law firm—someone I *am* involved with. I had a rather intense thing going with him, but have started backing off. The old pattern began to emerge—he began acting too possessive. I don't know if Paul's aware of him."

"Is this other man married?"

"No, he's not. And as far as I know, never has been. I like him—a lot—and would really like to continue seeing him but only with the understanding that I intend to see other men. I don't think he is handling the *other men* part of our relationship very well. His aggressive pursuit makes me a little nervous at times."

"You said *pursuit.* That gets very close to stalking."

"I'm sorry. Maybe I confused you. I like him, and I work with him every day. He isn't some annoying stalker. He's too possessive, but isn't that different?"

"There's such a fine line between stalking and being overly possessive. Most stalking victims don't recognize it in the beginning. Ann, one thing I do know is that if you are truly in danger from your husband, or from any of these other men, no one can protect you completely or forever. In other words, we have to eliminate the danger not just shield you from it. I'll start working on a plan to do that. In the meantime, you need to take extra precautions for your safety. Don't do anything that might set one of these guys off. That means forget dating for a while. Limit your activities to work, your visits to the WH Club, and your condo."

"Normally that would be easy for me. I don't have a long list of guys lining up at my door; but unfortunately, as cochair, I do have obligations involving the Swan Ball that I can't avoid."

"Okay, except for those must-do events, avoid things that might set your husband off."

"I understand, Mark."

"Do you have an alarm system at your condo?"

"Yes, and it's monitored."

"I want you to be sure to set it whenever you go out. When you are home, keep the doors locked and the alarm armed."

"Will do."

"Do you have a gun or some other weapon at your place?"

"Yes, actually I'm licensed to carry. Most lawyers are nowadays."

"What is it, and where do you keep it?"

"It's a LadySmith—a model 60LS revolver. It's a .38, but I keep it loaded with snake shot. It's in the top drawer of my bedside table."

"Ann, the danger is not from a snake. Reload your weapon with personal security ammunition. Do you have some hollow point ammunition?"

"Yes. I'll do what you say. I just thought the snake shot would stop someone without killing them."

"It might, but do you really want to leave that to chance? You have a real weapon. You need to arm it with real bullets."

"Okay."

"Until we can defuse the situation, it would be wise to get you some added security."

"You mean a bodyguard?"

"Let's just say someone to watch your back."

We ended our phone call. Had I misjudged who I'm dealing with? Was I being manipulated? Did she really want me to investigate the "murder" of her dog or was that just a pretense to get me involved with her men problems? I wasn't sure, but I promised I would do the dog thing so I had better get on it. First, however, I needed to call Bryan.

He answered almost immediately, "What's up, Chief?"

"I'll fill you in on the details later, but for now I need you to check on the whereabouts of one Paul Walton, an Emory University professor. Get all the info on him you can. What vehicles he drives, phone numbers, PDAs, etc."

"I'm on it, Chief."

"Good. Bryan, this needs to be your *numero uno* priority. As for number two, I want to know everything you can find out about some guy going by the name Lord Deed Millhouse."

"I take it you think this Lord Millhouse is not who he seems to be."

"He may be a stand-up guy, but I think I smelled a phony."

"I'll put one of our people on Millhouse. I'll work on the Walton guy myself."

"Perfect."

CHAPTER 9

Sam Littleton, FBI

"Mark, I would like to say it's good to hear from you, but my guess is that you've gotten yourself in trouble again. So cut to the chase. What can the FBI do for you today?"

Sam Littleton is the head of the FBI region that includes Nashville and a member of a joint agency task force dealing with Homeland Security. As for trouble, I thought about Walton's comment that he had me in his gunsight, but I decided now was not the time to mention that to Sam, at least not yet.

"I need a favor, old man, but it isn't about me this time. It's about a female lawyer who may be dealing with multiple stalkers. The main problem appears to be an abusive about-to-be ex-husband."

"That's not exactly FBI business, Mark."

"I'm working on the problem for her, Sam, but it is going to take a little time to ramp up. And in the meantime,

I would like someone on the federal side to provide her some personal protection."

"You want the FBI to be a babysitter?"

"Ann Sims is no baby, I assure you."

"Why do you need us?"

"She owns a gun and is licensed to carry. If she weren't a lawyer, she might be able to provide her own protection. But as it is, she has to go in and out of federal and state buildings and courts. You know that when it comes to federal buildings, civilians have to leave their hardware at home. You guys can carry your weapons inside. I want someone with firepower shadowing her until I can get my head around the situation. It doesn't have to be FBI. What about a marshal or someone from DEA or ATF? If you know someone with vacation time, I can make it worth their while."

"I don't want to get into facilitating moonlighting. She's a lawyer—an officer of the court. If you tell me she is in danger, then that's enough for me to allocate some manpower to this on a short-term basis. Anything more than a few days, however, and I will need something more substantial—drugs, terrorists, organized crime."

"That will work, Sam. How soon?"

"Give me a couple of hours. Do you have a phone number where we can reach her to work out the details?"

"Sam, you're a great guy. Thanks."

I gave him Sims's contact information and hung up the phone.

CHAPTER 10

Tony Caruso, Driver

After my early morning conversations with Sims and then Littleton, I joined Sarah for a later than usual breakfast. We watched the last of *Fox and Friends* and solved the world's problems during the commercials. By the time I had finished a quick shower, it was a little past nine o'clock. I was burning daylight fast and still had a busy day ahead. I called Tony, my driver, on the intercom to let him know he was needed.

I had driven myself to Ann Sims's last Friday but that was an exception. My Lexus—dubbed Black Beauty by the techno wizards' brain trust at the Women's Health Club— is a rolling computer and information center. The car also has armored sides and a few offensive weapons that are probably illegal. None of those features are of much use as long as I'm doing my own driving. That's why I have Tony Caruso.

Tony is an ex-submariner and an expert evasion driver. He is also a handy guy to have around in case of trouble. Unfortunately, trouble and I seem to cross paths regularly. Tony is quite a marksman, trained on multiple weapons. He owns a 9mm Glock but seldom carries it. For personal defense, he prefers an expandable tactical baton over a handgun. His preference is based on experience. According to Tony, the problem with a handgun is that it is deadly force. Good guys are not going to use deadly force unless they are actually under fire. One doesn't have the same reluctance about using a baton—you can render a bad guy completely helpless by breaking his wrist or shattering his kneecap with a single blow of a baton without putting innocent bystanders at risk from a stray bullet.

Tony lives in our guesthouse. Actually, it's more of a guest apartment—the second floor of an unattached supplemental two-car garage we had built a few years ago. The additional garage bays were to accommodate our growing fleet of golf carts used to drive around the property, some twelve acres that the family affectionately refers to as the "Rollins family compound." During the building process, Sarah decided that we might as well add a second-story guest apartment "just in case." I never figured out what the "just in case" was all about, but the additional living space turned out to be fortuitous. It enables us to keep Tony close by and available 24/7. Sarah had quarantined Tony last week because of a high fever and other nasty symptoms. I needed him back on the job and luckily the worst seemed behind him.

Tony brought Black Beauty around to the front of our house. I gave Sarah a peck on the cheek and got in the back of the Lexus. "Tony, the first stop is The Look, then lunch with my brother at Bricktops."

"Sure thing, Mr. R. You think the folks at The Look could work me in for a trim? Mrs. Rollins said I was beginning to look a little ragged. She doesn't like it when my hair starts hanging over my collar."

"They're usually booked, but you can always ask."

The Look hair salon is located in an older gray-white brick building on 22nd Avenue, just off Elliston. Elliston Place is an entertainment strip for locals, especially the Vanderbilt student community. It is where I go every couple of weeks to have two of my favorite ladies, Debbie and Heidi, make a new man out of me. The salon is not particularly large—seven chairs and one manicurist. It's spread over three narrow floors squeezed between a pizza shop on one end of the building and a neighborhood bar on the other. Debbie's chair is on the upper floor. Heidi, the manicurist, has her setup in the lower floor shared with the only male stylist. Don't let The Look's size or location mislead you. Their client list is impressive, including both male and female personalities from Nashville's music and entertainment community—some people you would immediately recognize and some important people who make things happen that you wouldn't know unless you were part of their world.

We arrived at 10:30 a.m. Tony was lucky. The ten o'clock color appointment for Linda, the owner of The Look, had been a no-show, so he took what was left of that scheduled appointment time. A walk-in, like Tony, getting a seat in Linda's chair is not standard operating procedure. In fact, it just doesn't happen, so I knew this was a favor to me. Everyone is always booked and there is a long waiting list for slots on their calendars—but Linda's waiting list is the longest. As one of her more famous patrons put it, "Linda is awesome at knowing the best cuts and color for you. She becomes your friend as well as your stylist."

The thing about The Look is that every member of the team has a unique personal style. They are artists and dress accordingly—no uniforms or smocks. Debbie shops at garage sales to put together a retro look. Her favorites are classic bowling shirts. Debbie's heritage is Native American. Her native name is Star Moon. She is tall with long, straight black hair, a handsome athletic build, and plays volleyball competitively.

Linda has wavy auburn hair and a curvy, girly figure. Heidi is a new member of The Look team. She's a young mother and part-time college student with a Bohemian spirit. She also grew up on a farm and has that farm girl clean, natural complexion that comes from favoring soap over foundation. Heidi replaced my previous manicurist, Annette, who recently moved to a salon closer to her home. I had been going to Annette for years before she moved; but in all that time, I think I had only seen her from the waist up, sitting behind her manicurist desk wearing her favorite *Men in Black* triangle-shaped wristwatch. Manicurists are good listeners. They are like bartenders. They listen to a lot of stories. It seems natural to sit at their table, surrender your hands, and immediately start telling your life story—or at least what you have been up to and up against since your last appointment.

When I was younger, men went to barbershops with red, white, and blue candy-striped poles near the entrances. Every place worth its salt had a manicurist and a shoeshine man. Both worked on you while you were having your hair cut. No one called it "styling" back then. Barber chairs were designed to accommodate the three-person grooming team. The barber stood behind you, the manicurist sat to the side of the chair on a small, short-backed, wheeled chair—something like an old-fashioned secretary's chair. There was a special tray for manicuring tools and a small metal pan of warm soapy water. The tray hooked into a slot built into the arm of the barber chair. Sometimes the shine man's shoe box had a built-in seat; if not, he used a very low stool while he worked his art, and popped his shine rag, at the foot of the barber chair.

Barbers' poles are gone for the most part. The shoe-shine men and boys have nearly disappeared. Many of the men I know don't get manicures. So why do I? Manicured nails, like a perfectly tailored suit, still convey a certain economic status. As the owner of the WH Club, I spend a lot of time dealing with the socially elite, wealthy women of Nashville. If you are not part of their glitterati world, in their eyes, you are invisible. In short, I have to look the part.

Believe it or not, my buzz cut takes about thirty minutes. Debbie starts with an electric trimmer using a number-one height guard on the top and sides, switches to a number two for the back, and then blends the two with scissors. Then we move to the shampoo station. After shampooing, it's back to the chair to do a search for any maverick hairs freed by the shampoo. A buzz cut leaves little room for error. One hair that sticks above my close-cropped field of salt and pepper changes the effect from well groomed to unkempt.

Heidi also does the nails of an author friend of mine. As she worked on me, she started laughing. She told me that my author friend was thinking about putting a crazed manicurist in one of his next books. The idea was that the manicurist hated men and had discovered a way to mix a slow-acting poison into the clear nail polish she used on her male clients. Heidi told the crazed man-hating manicurist story with such enthusiasm that I was glad I prefer to have my nails buffed—"No polish, thank you."

By 11:45 a.m., I was a completely new man, at least according to Debbie and Heidi. The restaurant where I was meeting my brother for lunch was only a couple of blocks away, and Tony still had fifteen minutes to get me there.

CHAPTER 11

Officer Butch Purdue, Badge Number 717

The sky opened in a torrential downpour right after I left The Look. The sky had that greenish look about it that usually foretells severe weather such as tornadoes. Tony got as close to the door of the restaurant, Bricktops, as he could, and I made a run for it.

Glen was already there. He had secured a booth in the bar area and was playing with his glass of red wine—probably a Pinot. I slid into the other side of the booth and used the large cloth napkin to towel off. Our server, a pretty girl with an Irish complexion and auburn hair pulled back in a ponytail, was standing next to our booth before I was completely settled. She looked familiar, and for good reason.

"Mr. Rollins, I don't know if you remember me. I'm Becky Ridder. I temped at Themis one summer while your receptionist was on pregnancy leave."

"Of course I remember you, Becky. You were a quick learner—did a good job. How have you been?"

"Okay, I guess. I decided to go back to school so I'll be enrolling at Middle Tennessee next semester."

"Good for you, Becky. MTSU is where I met my wife." I then nodded toward my brother. "Do you know my brother, Glen?"

Becky looked at Glen. "Gosh, I have waited on you for months but didn't know you two were related. I can see that now. Nice to know you by your name, Mr. Rollins."

"I'm Glen. That old guy on the other side of the booth is Mr. Rollins!"

Becky laughed. "*Mr.* Rollins, can I get you something to drink while the two of you decide on lunch?"

"Yes, a Skyy martini—straight up with olives."

Glen tapped his now-empty wine glass. Becky nodded. "Another glass of ZD?"

"Please."

"You got it. I'll be right back with your drinks and tell you about the specials."

Neither Glen nor I needed to look at the menu or hear about the specials. Creatures of habit we are. When Becky returned, Glen ordered his usual flatbread BBQ chicken. My standard fare at Bricktops is their Palm Beach salad—lump crabmeat, avocado, tomato, shrimp, and egg. Thankfully, my cholesterol can handle it.

After Becky walked away, I began my research. "Glen, do you know Ann Sims?"

"I do now. It was her dog that was killed in front of my condo. I was the one who called and gave her the bad news. The poor dumb animal was a regular."

"How is that?"

"He was just a big lovable lummox that showed up every morning to take a dump on our lawn. He was hit by a car—a Belle Meade police car of all things. But, the Sims woman has some responsibility for what happened. She always let that dog wander the neighborhood. We have a leash law in Nashville for good reason. I'm sure she is upset about it—probably spends some sleepless nights dealing with her own guilt. I know I would."

"Tell me what happened, Glen."

"When I'm in town, I walk my dogs on West End Avenue across from Montgomery Bell Academy every morning between 5:30 and 6:00. So just like Sims's dog, I'm a regular neighborhood fixture. People look for me— go out of their way to wave to us—me and my two dogs. Sims's dog was part of that ritual—day in and day out, my dogs and I were greeted by the big guy. I didn't know his name—Churchill—until after he was killed. He was a chocolate Lab. Unbelievably friendly—which was good, because given his size he could have used my two Shih Tzus as chew toys if he had wanted to.

"Anyway, it was just another morning. Churchill had done his thing. He got in a few Shih Tzu sniffs and a few pats from me. Then that big ol' lovable dog turned to trot back home across West End as he always did. He didn't see what I saw—a Belle Meade police car, far from its home base, no siren or flashing lights, but going like a bat out of hell. He was doing at least eighty—headed back toward Belle Meade.

"I can still hear the thud. I can still see the slow motion impact with flying pieces of metal and plastic from the car. The worst part—the absolute worst part, Mark—was watching Churchill, one hundred airborne pounds of brown fur, tumbling toward me. Churchill hit the curb, rolled, and landed against my legs. I froze. I couldn't move. I just stood there with a dead dog lying against my legs."

"Glen, I'm surprised. I hate to say it, but a car going that fast—I wouldn't have expected there to be much left of the dog, at least not in one piece."

"Ok, maybe I'm exaggerating the speed a little, but I'm telling you he was going way over the speed limit. The car caught him on the driver's side. Churchill must have jumped just before he was hit because he was thrown in the air."

"Did the driver stop?"

"The asshole tried to keep going. He finally stopped. But only because he saw us—me and the other people in their cars who witnessed what was beginning to look like a hit-and-run.

"There weren't a lot of cars on West End that early, but there were enough. Two of them pulled to the curb. One started backing up toward me. That's when the asshole decided he had better own up to running the dog down. He made a U-turn, turned on his flashing blue lights, and pulled up right next to me where I was still standing with that poor dead dog lying against my legs. The animal was bleeding all over the sidewalk. I was standing in his damn blood! The jerk, Officer Butch Purdue—badge number 717—actually smiled at me. He leaned over toward the passenger window and asked, 'Did I just hit that dog?' As if he didn't know! As far as I'm concerned, he was a macho jerk. You know the type—give them a gun, and they think they are God!

"I was seething—mad as hell—and told him as calmly as I could, 'I want your name and badge number. You were speeding—driving recklessly—*and* left the scene!' He tried to bully his way out of it—shouting at me. Said he was *not* speeding. When he saw that answer wasn't flying with me, he tried another one. The SOB actually said he was pursuing a speeding vehicle. I don't remember exactly what I said, but I made it damn clear I wasn't buying that shit! I wasn't stupid. He was a Belle Meade cop. He was in Metro where he had no business being. He was lying. I told him he had been speeding and had been clearly trying to leave the scene. The only thing that stopped him was that there were witnesses. He said, 'I'm calling my supervisor.' Then he put the vehicle's window up like a shield so I couldn't hear him talking to his station.

"Within five minutes, there were blue lights all over the damn place. By the end of this drama, there were no less than *six* police vehicles parked in front of our condo—four from Metro and two from Belle Meade. It looked like a major crime scene. They were closing ranks to protect that idiot—a wall of blue coming to the aid of a *fellow officer* facing an irate citizen demanding his badge number. Mark, it took *four* requests before the supervisor would give me Officer Purdue's name and badge number!"

"Glen, where was the culprit, Officer Purdue, while all that was going on?"

"Avoiding me, that is for sure! When he finally left the protection of his patrol car, Officer Purdue's first concern was not the dead dog. It was his stupid patrol car. He started trying to pull his fender back into place. My wife had joined me at the curb, and she said something to them about it. The supervisor, a young guy, smiled. It was a smart-ass smile. He said, 'Lady, it is not a crime for an officer to repair his car after an accident.'

"I had had it with those guys! I said 'I want to make a formal complaint against this officer.' The young cop said, 'Step aside,' like he was John Wayne. He started walking toward his car and over his shoulder said, 'If you wish to make a complaint, you'll have to do it at Belle Meade City Hall during normal business hours.' Just like that—no empathy whatsoever. I was just interference to them—someone complicating their day. I was a nuisance to be tolerated, but just barely. They rolled Churchill up in a tarp, put him in the trunk of one of the police cars, and left. All of that took about an hour."

"Glen, did you make a formal complaint?"

"Yes. My wife and I went back to the condo. I had breakfast and showered. I should have gone to my office because I had a lot going on that day, but I was still mad as hell. So instead, I drove directly to Belle Meade City Hall. Filled out their damn forms about the incident, including giving them the owner's name and address—your Sims woman. I had gotten that from the dog's tags. I figured nothing would happen if I stopped there. So I insisted on a meeting with the police chief, Carl Morgan."

"How did that go?"

"He was polite enough. I thought he was uncomfortable in his support of Officer Purdue, but he stood up for him. Morgan was not going to take just my word about the events. He said, 'This officer has a clean record, no complaints. You say he was speeding. He says he was not.

You say he was trying to leave the scene of the accident, but he didn't leave, did he?'

"I asked him if the patrol car had a video camera like most police cars nowadays. He admitted that it did, but said the camera has to be turned on by the officer or activated by turning on the lights. In this case, neither one of those things was in play. I asked for a copy of the accident report. He said the report wasn't available yet. Then he added, 'Look fellow, if your dog was hit, it was just an accident, but I will investigate the officer's conduct fully once I have the report from Metro.'

"Morgan hadn't read the forms I filled out—didn't even have the basic facts right about the incident. It wasn't my dog. I asked him when he thought he would complete his investigation. He told me he might be able to complete it by this time next week."

"And, that's where the two of you left it?"

"Mark, here is the deal. As far as Chief Morgan is concerned, *it was just a dog*! In his mind, I was the only one making a big deal out of this. All I wanted was for someone to take responsibility, show a little compassion. 'I'm sorry' would have gone a long way toward resolving this for me. No, Mark. *They* are the ones making it a big deal by trying to avoid responsibility. *They* are the ones who took *six* patrol cars and officers off-line to investigate *just a dog* getting hit by a car. *They* are the ones who are going to have a weeklong investigation over *just a dog*. I call it *Dog-Gate!*"

Becky brought our food. Glen was relieved to see it arrive. He is a true dog lover, and I could see that just retelling the story distressed him. We stopped talking dog. Glen had his ZD refilled and we concentrated on our lunch.

After we finished our entrees, Becky brought us coffee, and I ordered their key lime pie. Nashville is not known for its key lime pie, but Bricktops is an exception. Theirs reminds me of my mother's lemon icebox pie.

"Glen, do you mind if I stick my nose into this thing? Ms. Sims has asked me to look into Churchill's 'murder' as she calls it."

"I would be happy for you to jump in. I don't think I'm going to get any straight answers out of Morgan. He's playing rope-a-dope with me—stonewalling. I'm at the point of writing an editorial in the *Tennessean* about it. I doubt they would print it, but giving this incident public exposure is my best shot as a citizen of making sure Badge Number 717 gets what he deserves."

"Glen, I wouldn't be so down on Chief Morgan. Give him a chance to do the right thing. I know him, and he is a good man. I can understand that he doesn't want to judge his police officer prematurely. He has to support his man until he has collaborative evidence that Purdue acted improperly. My guess is that he will come down on the right side once he has all the investigative reports."

"What makes you think the reports will tell it like it was?"

"You said there were four Metro cars and two Belle Meade cars. Those guys are going to tell it like it was. I promise you. Yes, they will close ranks and provide support to a fellow officer in the line of fire—and that includes verbal fire from unhappy citizens. Like the chief, they start from an assumption that their man is innocent.

But they aren't going to falsify their reports. I've worked with too many of them to believe otherwise. In spite of how TV sometimes portrays these people, honor is their oath, and they don't tolerate bad apples in their midst."

"I hope you're right, Mark. I want that patrolman reprimanded, and he should have to personally pay for the damage to the police car."

"Glen, did you ever find out what Officer Purdue was doing outside Belle Meade's jurisdiction? What was he doing in Metro, and why was he in such a hurry to get back to Belle Meade?"

"No, I don't have that answer. I'm pretty sure he wasn't on official business. I suspect he was speeding in order to get back to Belle Meade before anyone discovered he was off the reservation. And Mark, before you meet with Chief Morgan, I want you to see this."

"What is that, Glen?"

Glen had his iPad in the booth. Apparently, he had been surfing the Web before I arrived. He turned the screen toward me. The Web page was the mission statement for the City of Belle Meade. Glen scrolled down to a section titled Values:

In carrying out its mission, the City of Belle Meade is guided by the following values:

Compassion – Empathy for the concerns of others.
Courtesy – Politeness in our dealings with others.
Creativity – Innovative solutions to problems.
Fairness – Consistent and equitable enforcement of the law.
Integrity – Strict adherence to moral and ethical principles.
Respect – Respect for the views, rights, and dignity of others.

Service – Prompt and competent service to others.

Teamwork – Trusting cooperation with other employees and residents.

Tolerance – Acceptance and support of diversity.

"Mark, you might want to remind the chief about some of those—especially the one about compassion."

CHAPTER 12

John Randall, Administrator

I t was Tuesday, a little before 1:00 p.m., in the law office of Chambers and White.

John Randall entered Ann Sims's office without stopping at the door to be invited. "Ms. Sims, do you have a minute for me?"

"Sure, but I do have to leave the office in about twenty minutes."

"I want to talk to you about your billable time."

"I know. I know—"

Randall, the law firm's administrator, is in his late thirties. He stands five feet ten inches and is very smart. Doctors recently discovered that he is allergic to wheat, which explained why he is so unusually thin. He had been on the audit staff of the national CPA firm Arthur Andersen.

Andersen was one of the Big Five accounting firms, including PricewaterhouseCoopers, Deloitte Touche Tohmatsu, Ernst & Young, and KPMG, but it was destroyed by its alleged role in the Enron affair. The Supreme Court later reversed the criminal conviction of the CPA firm, but it was too late. After surrendering its license, Arthur Andersen dissolved. It no longer exists.

Randall was disheartened after the firm's collapse. He wanted nothing more to do with the CPA profession. He applied for the administrator position with Chambers and White. The law firm, seeing a good thing, quickly hired him. As smart as he is, he was still a little insecure in his role as law firm administrator. By nature, he is mild-mannered. That puts him at a disadvantage in the challenging job of "herding cats"—which is how working with attorneys, especially law firm partners, has been described. Each thinks of himself or herself as an owner. Most have strong egos—high self-confidence bordering on obnoxious and overbearing. That can be a good thing when dealing with adverse parties, but it generally doesn't make for a congenial work environment.

John Randall was more or less a fish out of water, and he was also a pervert. He stood nervously in front of Ann's desk. That in itself was a problem. Ann stood five feet six inches at 120 pounds with a perfect hourglass figure. How he felt just looking at her made him feel guilty. It was the same feeling he got when peeping in the windows of the condos across from his.

He was in Sims's office to scold her. "Ms. Sims, I have everyone's time for the month except yours." He tried to raise the volume of his voice, but it only became more shrill. "I can't do my job as the firm's administrator without your time. The other partners blame me for not getting bills out fast enough. I look bad and the firm suffers.

When we don't get bills out on time, we don't get paid on time."

"Johnnie boy, I don't understand why it's such a big deal. Remember, Eli decided someone else should handle the Taylor thing? Well, he dumped it in my lap. Our fee is set by the court so it doesn't matter how much time I spend working on that matter. And everything else I'm working on is a negotiated fixed-fee arrangement."

The "Johnnie boy" stung. She was being dismissive. He would love to show her he was not Johnnie boy or any other kind of *boy*. "Ms. Sims, that doesn't matter. I still need everyone's time before I can close out the month. It's the firm's policy that everyone keeps track of their time in ten-minute increments and reports it. You are supposed to submit your time to me *daily*."

"My time isn't going to change anything, so if you're holding up billing because of me that is just a dumb policy."

"Ms. Sims, I *need* to have your time! Even if it doesn't change the bills this month, the court will eventually want to see how much time we spent on the Taylor estate matter before the judge releases the hold back."

"I hate keeping up with every ten minutes of my time. What do you want from me? You want me to play fill-in-the-blanks until I come up with enough billable time to satisfy you bean counters? In fact, maybe I'll make it look like I came in early, worked late, and only took fifteen-minute lunches. Give me a break, John!"

"Ms. Sims, that isn't the way it is anymore. You know that. We don't expect you to keep track of your time the old-fashioned way. The partners made a big investment to move us into twenty-first-century time tracking. We gave you and everyone else your choice of a BlackBerry or iPhone with the Carpe Diem time capturing system to make it easy. All you have to do is develop the habit of using it. It's very simple. It's easy for you, and we get your time automatically without having to wait until the end of the month. Carpe Diem lowers our cost and speeds up billing. You are a partner now. It puts more money in *your* pocket. I don't understand why you always fight me over this. *I need your time!*"

John Randall tried to lower the pitch of his voice. "Ms. Sims, I can't continue to cover for you. I am going to have to tell the partners that your failure to report your billable time in compliance with the firm's policy is the reason for delays in our billing."

"Look, Johnnie boy, you do that. I'm a big girl. I can handle the partners. I don't need you covering for me or giving me lessons on law firm profitability. I'll have your precious time to you by tomorrow morning, although it won't affect our profitability or partner income one little bit. Now, if you will stop staring at my breasts and leave my office, I will get to work earning those fees."

John's face turned beet red at the mention of breasts. *What did she expect? She wore those tight, clinging tops—she wants me to look.* The truth is, he hoped she would always be late submitting her time. Then he could come to her office, stare at those lovely breasts, and scold her. Maybe she liked that too. Maybe that's why she was always late.

— ✄ —

Before leaving her office, Ann dialed Eli's extension. "I'm going to the Taylor mansion to look over the property. I want to make sure it's ready for the auction. It's about lunchtime. Do you want to grab a sandwich and ride out to the Taylor place with me? You might be interested in some of the antique stuff."

"Sorry, babe, I can't—having lunch with a client. But why are you going out there? The auction is on track. It is on the calendar just a few more days from now. All you need to do is make sure the paperwork is complete. We have no responsibility regarding the property itself. Save yourself the trouble."

"I just thought I'd check. However, there's another reason for calling you. A few minutes ago I had a little run-in with our persnickety administrator. You might have to run a little interference for me. He's going to tattle on me to the other partners."

"John? What about?"

"He was trying to bully me for not getting my time in. I think the little creep just wanted to ogle me. I caught him staring at my breasts the whole time he was talking."

"That little creep—I should cut off his balls and make him eat them."

"I don't think he's really dangerous, but he *is* kind of weird—and so thin. He reminds me of that man in the Halloween story, the one about the teacher and the headless horseman."

Eli laughed. "You mean Ichabod Crane from *Sleepy Hollow.*"

"Yes, that's who I mean—old Ichabod."

"Ann, don't worry about Ichabod, I'll take care of the boy. But what is your problem? The Carpe Diem system is really easy. We're capturing more billable time than ever. Our realization is up more than thirty thousand dollars per attorney. That's real money, babe. You're the only holdout. Even the old guys are okay with it. So what is it with you?"

"I don't know. Maybe it's a feminist thing. We have to exert ourselves. You know, to show how tough we are, or maybe I just don't like doing what some skinny administrator tells me I have to do. I'm an attorney, goddamn it!"

"Ann, if you would just start using the tools we've given you like the rest of us, you wouldn't have to deal with John's harassing you."

"I doubt that. I get the feeling that he gets off on scolding me. If I changed my habits—became anal about getting my time in—he would probably just find some other excuse to undress me with his eyes."

"Hey, babe, that's *my* favorite sport! I don't want that pipsqueak playing on my turf! He needs to keep his eyes off my property. I told you not to worry about him, babe."

"Thanks for watching my back. It's important to know you're in my corner."

"Well, you may really need my help if you go through with your plan this weekend. What if this guy isn't exactly magnanimous? He could cause a lot of trouble for you. You could find yourself in front of the disciplinary board, or worse, you know."

"I don't have any choice. He made it clear that he wouldn't be put off any longer."

Eli said nothing.

"Eli, are you still there?"

"Yeah, babe, I was thinking."

"I admit I'm scared. I've always been afraid it would come out. At least this way, I pick the timing. I just have to hope the money will be enough for him."

— ✦ —

Betty Foster, the receptionist, shouted at Sims as she was going out the door of the law firm. "Ms. Sims, I have Ann Sparrow on the phone for you."

"Betty, just take a message."

"She says it's very important—that she is calling at the request of a Mr. Rollins."

"I can't take it now, Betty. I've been trying to get out of the office for the last hour. You can give her my home phone number. Tell her to call me at home tonight."

Betty whispered wide-eyed, "She said she was calling from the FBI office. What about your cell phone? You could talk to her while driving."

Ann grimaced. "Damn. Maybe I created a monster by talking to Rollins."

"What did you say, Ms. Sims?"

"Nothing, Betty. I was talking to myself. Just tell her you couldn't catch me and you don't know where I am. But give her my home number and suggest she call me at home tonight."

Sims didn't wait for a reply from the receptionist and was out the door before Betty could say anything more.

CHAPTER 13

Bryan Gray, WHC's Chief of Technology

The Lexus was parked against the curb directly in front of the restaurant door. Tony was standing by the rear passenger door waiting for me as Glen and I exited the building. He opened the door, and I slid inside and gave my brother a good-bye salute. The rain had stopped for now. May is one of those months when anything is possible weather-wise. I was glad the greenish cast was gone. The sky was clear. The forecast coming over the radio wasn't for clear weather, however. The announcer was explaining that a slow-moving front was headed our way and was making it sound pretty ominous.

"Tony, take us home by way of the WH Club. It'll be a quick stop."

"Roger that, Mr. R."

My to-do list was growing. Getting to that list was complicated by the fact that I had an important appointment the next day in DC. The first item on the list was 24/7 protection for Sims. Thankfully, Littleton's agreement to watch her back gave me the time I needed to keep my DC appointment. His coverage was only a stopgap measure, however. I still needed a more permanent plan. Then there was the needed sit-down with Chief Morgan about the so-called murder of Churchill. As for other items on the list, they depended in part on what Bryan and his team could dig up while I was gone. We needed to determine what we were dealing with as far as Lord Deed Millhouse was concerned. Another top priority was finding a way to keep tabs on the movements of Sims's about-to-be former husband, Paul Walton.

Flying into our nation's capital had become problematic. The only commercial flights allowed to fly into Reagan International are small jets with seats designed for midgets and adolescents. From Nashville, Baltimore via Southwest is an alternative, if you don't mind the hour-plus drive into the District. While Southwest flies full-size planes and scores high marks when it comes to on-time performance, no full-size adult would ever describe a Southwest flight as anything more than tolerable—due again to crowded, undersized seats. After considering my alternatives, I did the only logical thing. I called Stratos Jet Charter Service from the car and ordered up a Challenger 300 for the trip. The Challenger is a Bombardier product classified as a super-midsize aircraft. It has a range of three thousand miles at five hundred miles per hour, and most importantly, measuring more than seven feet, it has one of the widest cabins of any private jet in its class. By chartering the Challenger, I could make the trip in one day by avoiding security lines and long airport waits.

I was about to make another call to arrange for a car and driver with Boston Coach when I received a message on Black Beauty's computer display. Surprisingly, it was from A1 Omega Limo Service of DC. "We understand you are arriving in DC tomorrow via a Stratos charter. A car will be waiting for you compliments of Signore Greco."

Since I had helped his son out of some trouble, the don mysteriously manages to keep track of my travel plans. Whenever I fly into New York, one of his drivers is always waiting for me as I step off the plane. The restrictions on non-passengers in the concourse never seemed to stop Signore Greco from having his man at my gate.

Having a driver meet me in Washington was a first, however. Apparently the New Jersey don was expanding his operations into the District.

If you are involved in slightly shady business activities, operating a limo service has a number of advantages. A lot of transactions are made in cash, making it an ideal money laundering setup. Illegal proceeds can be recycled as cash revenues of the limo service. Reporting the revenues as legitimate business income and paying taxes on it keeps the Feds off your back. The limo service is also a feeder business. Limo clients are often referred to other enterprises owned or sponsored by the family—including perfectly respectable restaurants, as well as escort services, backroom gambling establishments, and drugs.

My don only deals in recreational stuff—"no heroin or cocaine" according to Signore Greco himself. For me to refuse his offer of the complimentary car service would be an insult. And one has to be careful about insulting a Mafia boss, even one like Signore Greco who has transitioned away from heavy crimes into simply shady or only slightly illegal activities.

I was traveling to DC to meet with a former navy admiral and his business partner, an ex-CIA spook. Before retiring, Raymond Arkwright had worn three stars in the navy as a vice admiral and Chief of Naval Operations for Information Dominance. Charles Newhouse was a black ops man who got burned. His cover destroyed, he left the CIA but continues to ply his clandestine skills. Only now he earns big bucks for his services.

Why did they want to meet with me? There is a lot more to the Women's Health Club than meets the eye. Out of sight from the club's clientele of wealthy women and young trophy wives is one of the nation's most powerful computer and information centers. It's attended by my brain trust, a very smart team of loyal techno geeks. They were part of my team at Vector Data and then Themis Legal Software. It seemed the admiral and the spook wanted to use our services on behalf of a client who lost billions in the structured securities auction market. The challenge, on behalf of their client, was to prove that the large international financial house was selling the securities to their client at the same time it was dumping its own investment portfolio in anticipation of a collapse in the structured securities market.

The admiral's team was engaged in a search for a smoking gun somewhere in millions of documents, e-mails, and text messages that had been turned over to them through legal discovery. Finding that smoking gun in the discovery documents would be relatively easy if they still existed. If the bad guys were smart—and they were—such incriminating evidence probably didn't exist any longer—at least not in the discovery documents. That's why the admiral's people needed my services. Unscrubbed incriminating evidence was more likely to exist somewhere in the *triacontatrillions* of ones and zeros in the ether of the World Wide Web.

If I took the job, it would be the first time the WH Club had taken on contract work for a nongovernmental entity. No one, aside from a select few government agencies, knows about our intelligence gathering capabilities. We are a better kept secret than the super-secret National Security Agency, the NSA. We just don't operate in the commercial world. So why was I meeting with these people? The very fact they knew about us was remarkable and reason enough to want to know more about them. Also, these guys were waving a five million dollar nonrefundable retainer under my nose with a twenty million dollar back-end contingent fee if we succeeded. It's the kind of offer you almost can't refuse.

Another message popped up on the car's display. This time it was an incoming call from the headman of my brain trust, Bryan Gray. Bryan's official title as an employee of the WHC is Chief Technology Officer.

"What's up?"

Long ago, Bryan and I began skipping the phone niceties, which we both viewed as a waste of time. He quickly learned I prefer to get to the point.

"Chief, I have no idea where your man Paul Walton is."

"You couldn't track his cell phone?"

"The guy must be a battery puller. As long as the battery is out, the guy is invisible. He puts it back in when he needs to make a call. Keeps the call short and pulls the battery again. That is all we can figure."

"That computes based on the little bit of information Ann Sims has already told me. He got into the protest movement back in college. Those people are paranoid types—concerned that Big Brother is always watching. He probably learned how to keep from being tracked in the movement. Although, I don't think they had cell phones back then."

"Chief, these people stay in touch and update their skills. It's easy enough today with blogs and websites."

"Good point, and the fact that he knows how and that he is using those stealth techniques makes him a dangerous man."

"Amen! So we're falling back on old-fashioned detective work. I called the university and asked to speak to him. They connected me to his office, but all I got was a voice mailbox. I left a message that sounded like a job offer—a call I would have expected him to return; however, there has been nothing from him thus far. I also have some contacts on the ground. They checked his place, and neighbors haven't seen him for three or four days. I had one of my guys call the university again and used the family emergency ploy. We were advised that the professor is on leave and not expected to return until the end of the month."

"They give you a reason?"

"Not officially, but we kept nosing around. He has graduate students covering his classes. We got to one of them, and he said he understood it was for personal reasons—an illness in the family. I guess our missing person is also using the old family emergency ploy."

"What about his car?"

"The only one we know about is still parked at his condo in Georgia."

"Then he has to have rented a car."

"We have checked the rental companies, and if he is renting, it's under an assumed name. You wouldn't normally expect a college professor to have the knowledge and wherewithal required to do that—you know, you have to have an ID, credit cards, etc. Now that I know about his extracurricular college activities, I believe I may have underestimated him."

"Maybe not. I have an idea, Bryan. Check for a motorcycle. He could have borrowed one or purchased it privately. He has to be staying somewhere, and my guess is he's staying as close to Ann Sims as he can. Check motels, working outward using her place as the center of your search circle. Look for someone on a motorcycle."

"We'll give it a shot, Chief. I also have something else for you."

"What's that?"

"Your lady is about to come into quite a fortune—more than enough to give someone a motive for murder."

"Bryan, don't hold me in suspense."

"Sims, her parents, and her best friend were in a terrible car wreck just on the other side of Monteagle. Ann was the only survivor. She was around sixteen at the time—an only child. Her parents were moderately wealthy. The estate was worth about six million dollars and the parents had one of those spendthrift clauses in their wills. All of the money is to be held in trust until age thirty-five. The trustee is Goldman Sachs, and they've been pretty generous in providing for her—the best schools, money for the condo, car, etc. The point is she hasn't suffered for a lack of access to money and for good reason—Goldman has the Midas touch. The trust that terminates pretty soon is worth something close to sixty million dollars. That's a tenfold increase in just under twenty years—not a bad return on investment."

"What happens if Sims dies before she reaches thirty-five?"

"That is the reason for concern. The entire fortune would go to her father's brother, Eugene Sims, who lives in DC. He worked in the Bush administration and, of course, is out in the cold now that the Democrats are in. I ran credit reports. He appears to have lost his shirt in the stock market when the housing bubble burst. Now he works for one of the conservative think tanks in DC, but Uncle Eugene has *a lot* of debt on his shoulders."

"Are you tracking his whereabouts?"

"Yep, and guess where your man is."

"You're kidding."

"He is right here in Music City—attending the Tea Party convention at the Gaylord Opryland Hotel. He's a delegate."

"Good work, Bryan. I think I should pay Mr. Sims a visit. Get his cell phone number for me. While you are at it, lock onto his cell phone and send that connection to the GPS app on my iPhone."

"Sure thing, Chief, but he's likely to be in meetings during the day."

CHAPTER 14

The Tapestry

Ann wandered through the derelict mansion. Impressive in its day, the old house was a relic, a museum, an antique—interesting but useless.

The house stood exactly as it was built in the 1930s. Neither Taylor nor his wife had made any improvements or changes during their lifetime, except one. They had installed a speaker and an electrical gate control to limit who was allowed in or, more specifically, who Mr. Taylor could keep out. Now the dusty old house had sat unoccupied for more than fifty additional years. Perhaps if Taylor had used a word other than *preservation* in his handwritten will, things would be different. But he hadn't, and the executor had followed those brief instructions to the letter. The doors were locked just as Taylor was laid to rest in Woodlawn Memorial Park beside his loyal wife. William and Mildred Walker, along with other remaining domestic staff were exiled to the bunkhouse. The old mansion had been "preserved" and, except for the additional fifty-plus years of dust and decay, remained the same as the day the old man's body was carted away by the medical examiner. Now, in spite of its grand facade, the house that Taylor had built was a tear down of little value—its rehabilitation too expensive, and for zero lot developers it was an obstacle to be removed quickly before preservationist tried to prevent it.

Its timeworn fixtures and furniture belonged to a bygone era. There were no closets. Bathrooms were small and utilitarian. The heavy velvet window treatments were original to the house. The wooden floors, stiffened by time, popped and creaked as Ann explored the old house. The floors were stained dark and covered by rugs laid down more than eighty years ago.

Why were the fireplaces so small? She looked closer at the one in the dining room and understood. A small brass bin next to the fireplace was embossed with the word COAL. She also realized that there was no central heat and, of course, no air conditioning.

Ann moved on to the kitchen. It was a 1930s version of a commercial kitchen. Pots and pans were large and dull, like those Ann assumed were used in restaurants. There were two sinks—both were unusually deep. She noticed there was no dishwasher. Everything must have been washed by hand in those sinks. There was a butcher's block table in the center of the room. Apparently, meat was purchased in bulk and cut in portions here. The kitchen was clearly a workplace, never intended to be used by the lady of the house.

There was a large butler's pantry that opened off the kitchen. She found an old-fashioned fuse box inside like those she had seen in classic black-and-white movies. The wooden box, built like a shallow cabinet with a glass door, was mounted on the wall with electrical wires running from the ceiling down to the top of the box and from the box down through the floor. Walking from room to room, she had noticed how few electrical outlets there were. Even the lighting was sparse and there were no electrical appliances to speak of, only an occasional fan and one old radio. Looking at the fuse box, she suspected the wiring was unsafe.

Out of curiosity, she opened the box's glass door. On the inside of its wood frame was a key hanging on a small nail. The key was old and it looked odd. She reached in her jacket pocket for the key that Eli had given her—the one she had used to enter the house. She was right. The key in the fuse box was definitely different. She took it off the hook and turned it over in her hand. Perhaps it was the key to one of the other buildings—maybe the carriage house.

Not satisfied with her own answer, she looked around the pantry. It was eight feet wide and twice as deep—like a wide hallway. There were shelves on each side. At the end of the room, farthest from Ann, there were no shelves. A tapestry hung from near the ceiling and reached all the way down to the floor. She walked over and ran her hand slowly across it. It might be silk and was probably beautiful in its day, but time and neglect had taken its toll. She studied the scene—a French countryside with grapevines and baskets of freshly picked grapes. It must have been valuable. Why would anyone hang something like this in a place where no one would see it? She looked at the key in her hand and then at the tapestry. She remembered her conversation with Judy about a secret room.

She spoke out loud: "Are you hiding something, Howard?" She pulled the tapestry to one side. "Aha! You are, aren't you? Well, Mr. Taylor, let's see what secrets you have hidden behind this door!"

CHAPTER 15

The Secret Room

A combination of excitement and apprehension filled Ann's chest as she stood in front of Taylor's tapestry-covered secret door. What had he been hiding?

It was not a standard-size door. It was shorter and wider. It was not flimsy. It was built out of heavy timber—maybe 4 by 6 lumber. It reminded her of the door to her grandmother's root cellar, only this door was much stronger. It probably led to some additional storage area or to a storm cellar. *But then,* she wondered, *why hide that behind an expensive tapestry?* Maybe it was a panic room—a place to store valuables or hide from danger. She tried the key in the door's lock. It turned, and the door opened easily. That surprised her.

The light from the pantry spilled onto steps leading down into darkness. *It must be a basement room,* she thought. There was not enough light to see to the bottom of the stairs. Glad the electricity had been turned on in preparation for the auction, Ann searched for a light switch. She felt along the wall inside the stairway. Her hand touched an old-fashioned knob switch like those in the rooms she had already explored. She began to turn it. The lights glowed, then slowly brightened. Curiosity gripped her.

She started down the long steep stairs. They had been cut out of hard Tennessee granite. She held tightly to the cold iron railings on both sides of the stairs. *Unusual,* she thought, *like small railroad tracks.* She looked up and saw a circle of rust-colored wire cable running along the ceiling. Ann was baffled at first but then made it out to be part of an old pulley system. She realized that rather than banisters, they were tracks used to lower and raise whatever was down below. She soon saw that the stairs ended on a platform cut out of the same granite as the steps. Apparently, the cellar room that the stairs were leading her toward was at a right angle to the platform because she could still not see anything below other than the ending of the stairs. It was a loading platform, and, as she got closer, she saw the device that must have run on the tracks—a metal wagon that reminded her of scenes in movies, only this wagon was smaller. It was a miniature version of a railcar—like those used to haul coal out of a mine.

Ann had no idea what secret she was about to uncover, but the excitement of discovery tinged with some fear of the unknown quickened both her breathing and the beating of her heart. She slowly reached the platform. Not knowing what to expect, it took several seconds for her mind to fill in the blanks—when it had, she whispered out loud—"My God, it is *wine*—it is full of wine!" Her voice echoed. She talked to the echo, "This place is *enormous!*"

She quickly stepped off the platform and began walking through the stacks of wine in amazement. The room was cool and dry. The wine bottles were in perfect condition. How long had they been there—undisturbed?

The cellar reminded her of the catacombs in Rome. The room was at least twenty feet across. There were shelves—large diamond- and box-shaped bins—from floor to ceiling on each of the outer walls. Then down the center, running for no less than sixty feet, were two more of the same wooden shelves set back-to-back. The labels on the wine bottles were in French. The layers of bottles on the top of some bins were covered in dust. Others looked as if the wine had been laid down yesterday. That surprised her too. She picked up one of the bottles. The label read *Château Pétrus 1929*.

When she got to the end of the room, there were unopened wooden cases stacked from wall to wall—twenty feet of cases, four and five cases high, and three rows deep! Ann was not a wine person, but she recognized some of the names branded into the wooden cases. There were cases of *Château Latour* as well as *Mouton* and *Lafite Rothschild*. She also saw *Château Margaux* and *Château d'Yquem*. There were others—too many to remember.

CHAPTER 16

Agent Ann Sparrow, Bodyguard

Now my display screen indicated an incoming call from Sam Littleton.

"Hello, Sam. What's up?"

"Your lady friend seems to be avoiding us. I assigned Agent Sparrow as the lead to cover her 24/7 until we can turn this babysitting job back over to you, but we seem to be having a problem catching up with her. She isn't taking our calls. Any ideas?"

"Let me try calling her. I'll get back with you."

Ann answered my call on the third ring. "Ann, this is Mark Rollins."

"I'm so glad you called! I've made an extraordinary discovery and can't wait to tell someone about it."

"Save it for later. Right now, I'm concerned with saving your skin. Why aren't you taking the calls from Agent Sparrow?"

"Who?"

"You asked me to keep you alive. Sparrow is part of the team set up to do that."

"Oh, so that's who she is. I've been so rushed today. I didn't want to get tied up with someone on the phone. I have to get this property ready for the auction."

"Where are you?"

"I'm at the old Taylor place on Hillsboro Road."

"Don't go anywhere until Sparrow gets there."

"Mark, maybe I was too paranoid about this. You really think I need a bodyguard?"

Sims obviously had buyer's remorse. But I had taken on the job and didn't like the things that were surfacing—a stalking husband, jealous lovers, an angry Belle Meade policeman, plus an uncle short on money and in line to inherit a fortune. "Look, Ann, right now I can only go on what little I have been able to find out and what you have already told me. And that is enough to tell me that, *yes*, you need protection!"

"Maybe I was overreacting."

I didn't want to increase the scare factor, but I needed her to get real and get with the program. "There is one way to find out for sure."

"Oh?"

"Yes, we can do nothing. If Paul or one of these other guys murders you, we will know for sure then, won't we? Does that sound like a workable plan for you?"

"Of course not."

"Okay then. It's time for you to stop making our job of keeping you alive more difficult."

Ann knew there was only one correct answer, but she also decided not to tell Rollins about her discovery, at least not yet. So she said, "Okay, I promise." She made it sound apologetic.

— ♪ —

After getting Ann's commitment to the plan, I called Sam back. "Sam, she's at the Taylor mansion on Hillsboro Road, or maybe it's Hillsboro Pike—the name changes somewhere around Forest Hills."

"I know the place, Mark. Sparrow should be able to get there within an hour and a half or maybe a little less. Make sure Sims *stays put*."

"Oh, she'll be there."

— ♪ —

While she waited, Ann sat in the small study of the old house, excitedly going over the list she had made. The more she thought about it, she wished she had told Rollins about the wine. She had heard that he knew a lot about these things. But there was someone else who knew about wines. She picked up her iPhone, found his phone number, and called.

"Hello."

"Hello. It's Ann Sims."

"My dear, it is so nice to hear from you. I wasn't sure I would have the chance to see you again before I returned to London."

"You remember we talked about the auction I was working on?"

"Yes, the Taylor place. I may still decide to bid on that as an investment. In fact, I drove by it yesterday."

"Well, I have found something that may change everything, but I need someone like you to look at it. It may make a big difference in the estate's value, but I'm not an expert. Can you come by the property?"

"Sounds intriguing. I'm just leaving Nero's Grill in Green Hills. I had a nice lunch with the people from your symphony. It seems they would like to be included in my charitable donations."

"Then you are only two minutes away. I really need your advice."

"Okay, I'm turning right on Hillsboro and will be there in a flash."

"Wonderful! What I have to show you will be quite a surprise."

CHAPTER 17

Eugene Sims

Tony changed our course. We headed for the Opryland Hotel. Actually, that's not its name anymore. After the Gaylord family purchased the property, they changed its name to Gaylord Opryland. Their marketing literature refers to it as Gaylord Opryland Resort and Convention Center. To locals, it is still simply the Opryland Hotel.

Traffic was terrible. Our stimulus dollars were at work repairing potholes.

The display indicated another call from Sam.

"Yes, Sam?"

"Well, the plot thickens, my friend!"

"How so?"

"I sent one of my people to Sims's condo to stand by until we were sure Agent Sparrow had your lady in tow. It turned out we are not the only ones looking after her."

"What do you mean?"

"Metro had a black-and-white parked in front of the complex. We checked on it. We were told by Metro that higher-ups had the car deployed to the condo at the request of Chief Morgan of Belle Meade—a personal favor, chief to chief."

"Any ideas, Sam?"

"I can guess. You told me that Sims and her dead dog are at the center of a complaint against one of his officers. I would say Morgan must have come down on her side— decided that the complaints were justified and fired the man. Now the chief is worried that his ex-officer might just take his anger out on civilians, including Ms. Sims."

"Sounds believable; I'll check with Chief Morgan and find out what is what."

"Okay. Should I keep my man there?"

"No, for now let's let Metro handle the sentry duty."

As Sam and I ended our phone call, Tony was pulling up to the Magnolia entrance of the hotel. Opryland still receives incoming guests at this older lobby, but most arriving guests check in at the newer Cascades entrance. But I wasn't checking in.

A uniformed doorman opened my door. "Checking in, sir?"

"No. I'm just meeting someone." I handed him a twenty-dollar bill and said, "Please show my driver where he can wait."

"Sure thing, sir."

I left Tony and the doorman to work out the arrangement as I began my search for Eugene Sims by calling the cell phone number Bryan had texted me.

Sims answered his phone but apparently dropped it in the process. After a few seconds and some clattering noise, a voice whispered, "Hello?"

"Mr. Sims, my name is Mark Rollins. I would like to talk to you about your niece, Ann Sims."

"Just a second. I'm in a meeting. Let me go out to the hallway." After about a minute and in a normal voice, he said, "Okay, I can talk now. I had forgotten to silence my phone, and your call came right in the middle of a presentation by Tom Tancredo."

"Sorry about that."

"It wasn't your fault. I'm the guilty party. But forget that, you mentioned my niece."

"Yes. You know she lives here in Nashville?"

"Yes, of course. In fact, I'm meeting her while I'm here. It will be the first time I've seen her since the accident. What is your connection with Ann, and how did you know I was here?"

"Ann believes she may be in danger and asked me to provide personal security for her."

"Oh, my . . . surely you don't think I would harm her!"

"You are aware of the provision in your brother's trust fund making you the beneficiary in the event of her untimely death?"

"I haven't thought about that document in almost twenty years. I firmly believe the money belongs to Ann, not to me. I can make my own way in this world."

"Why now?"

"What do you mean?"

"You said this will be the first time you'll be seeing her since the accident. Why are you meeting with her now when you went all those years without setting eyes on her?"

"That was *her* doing. I have tried to stay connected with her since my brother's death, but she rejected all my attempts. I never knew why. Every time I tried to visit her, she made some excuse. I thought it was very strange, and I finally told her so."

"When was that?"

"Twice, really. I tried to talk to her a few months ago when I was sure I would be a delegate here. She was still making vague excuses about getting together. Finally, I decided to confront her just before this trip so I left a message on her answering machine. I made it clear that she is family—has the same blood as me in her veins—and that she owes me the courtesy of seeing me while I'm in town and at least staying in touch. You know what I mean . . . calling or sending cards for birthdays and holidays like Christmas and Thanksgiving. I didn't expect her to treat me as a father. I told her if she didn't agree to meet me, I would camp out at her law office until she did. She finally called me back and told me I was being silly. Of course she would meet with me. So when the convention wraps up, I'm staying over an extra day. Ann and I have a date for dinner at a place called Whitfield's."

He appeared to have been deeply hurt by Ann's continued rejection of him. I couldn't rule out the possibility that he was faking it, but I was growing less concerned about his appearance in Nashville.

"You know, Mr. Rollins, I loved that little girl. I used to visit my brother for several weeks every summer. Ann and I became very close. My brother's death sent me to bed. Depression. I couldn't go to the funeral. Didn't visit Ann in the hospital. I assume she hated me for that, but I just couldn't help it. I still carry a picture of Ann and me in my billfold that was taken on her fourteenth birthday. I can't tell you how eager I am to see her again. I am blathering, aren't I? I'm sorry. You said she is in danger?"

"She is concerned about her safety."

"Is it something related to her work? She's a lawyer, you know. Oh, I'm sure you know that. Tell me what I can do. I so want to help."

"You have already helped me. Can I buy you a cup of coffee or a beer? I would like to meet you face-to-face."

"Okay. Any suggestions? This is your town."

"I'm already in the hotel, so I suggest Rusty's. It's the sports bar in the Magnolia Lobby."

"Yeah, I know where it is. Give me about fifteen minutes. I need to stop by my room for a quick visit, and then I'll join you. Oh, I'm wearing a bow tie. There aren't many of us bow-tie people around, so you shouldn't have a problem recognizing me."

We ended our call.

I was already standing in front of the bar. The hostess gave me a table where I could face the door to watch for Eugene. I had time to call Bryan back.

"Hello, Chief. You find your man okay?"

"Yes, thanks. I need you to jump on something else for me. I'm not sure, but we could have an *ex*–Belle Meade patrolman looking to take his anger out on our client, Ann Sims. I will explain later. For now, what I need is for us to track him so we can make sure he isn't trying to get close to Ms. Sims."

"Give me his name, rank, and serial number, and we will take it from there, Chief."

"I'll give you what I have." I had written down his name and badge number while at lunch with Glen. "The only name I have is Butch Purdue. It's an easy guess that Butch is just a nickname. His badge while he was on the force was 717. Once you start tracking him, contact Mariko. If it looks like our man is on the hunt for Sims, I want Mariko ready to head him off at the pass."

"Roger that!"

"Thanks, Bryan." I clicked off.

When the server appeared, I ordered my favorite, a Skyy martini, straight up with olives. I don't like the lemon garnish that seems to be the preferred way vodka martinis are served nowadays. The sports bar's TVs were tuned to C-SPAN, which was covering the convention in the hotel—probably because Sarah Palin was scheduled to speak to the group later in the day. The convention was turning into a planning session as the Tea Party laid out its strategies for taking back Congress from the "radicals," as the Tea Party leaders called the regime now in power. I don't know if the label is right, but we do have a House of Representatives and, to a lesser extent, a Senate that is not listening to the voters. The current Democrats in power seem totally out of touch with the wishes of the people they represent.

I looked at my watch and saw that the fifteen minutes were up. Just then a tall, thin man dressed like a dandy glided into the bar. I waved him over. He was wearing skinny black jeans, a black vest over a striped dress shirt, complete with a yellow bow tie with small red hearts.

When he sat down and crossed his long legs, I saw he had Roper boots with three-inch heels—probably Lucchese or at least handmade. The boots were unusual since Ropers are usually low-heeled boots. He was breathing hard as he said, "Need to catch my breath . . . you have to walk a mile to get anywhere in this hotel. It's a great place, but I wish they had moving sidewalks."

"Thank you for meeting me, Mr. Sims. What will you have?"

"A Michelob Ultra."

I signaled the server, a young man named John Holzapfel, and ordered the beer. Holzapfel was trying to break into the music business and, like many other aspiring entertainers, worked as wait staff around town and for local caterers. I recognized him as one of the bartenders who had worked a catered event Sarah hosted recently for one of the local charities she supports.

Sarah and I had donated the wine for the event and Holzapfel impressed me with the care he took to avoid opening bottles before they were needed. That way, the unused wine could be returned for a refund. Most of the people who work wine bars at catered events couldn't care less. They pop the corks on everything they have in inventory to make their job pouring easier. A lot of good wine is wasted. As a wine lover, I hate to see that happen.

After the requisite social nonsense, Sims continued, "I would like to know more about this danger Ann is supposed to be facing."

"Sure. Do you know about her divorce?"

"She mentioned it on the phone."

"It's about to become final. She was in an abusive marriage, and her estranged husband seems to be stalking her."

"How awful! I'm so sorry to hear that. You know, I just don't know much about Ann's recent life. She didn't even invite me to her wedding. In fact, she and I have not talked for a total of ten minutes since the accident—at least until this week. And even then, I did most of the talking."

"Frankly, Mr. Sims, I wanted to make sure that you were not a threat."

"Me? For heaven's sake—no, no, no. I'm a lover, not a killer."

"Come now; let's be honest. If something happened to your niece, you would inherit quite a lot of money. And I know that you are not in the best financial shape right now."

"So you have been checking up on me. Well, yes—but I've been behind the eight ball before and have always come back. I'll come back this time. I have some very rich friends who know how to make money. Hell, they practically run the printing press at the Fed. The market is still a rigged game, and they run the tables. They have let me in on deals before, and they'll do it again. Trust me. I don't need Ann's money."

"I think I believe you, Mr. Sims, but just in case I'm wrong about you—and I'm not wrong very often—keep in mind your niece is under my protection. If anything happens to her, I will see to it that the person who harms her pays for it severely."

"You don't mince words, do you, Mr. Rollins? I think you just gave me a compliment and threatened me at the same time. But let me assure you that I'm on your side, or, I should say, Ann's side."

CHAPTER 18

Fiduciary Duty

Lord Millhouse and Ann were standing under the mansion's *porte-cochère.*

"Ann, I need to say it again—this is an extraordinary find!"

"Yes, Deed, but what about its value? I need to get with the heirs and the judge handling it. They need to decide how to handle this new development before the auction details are finalized. As it stands right now, a buyer will have the opportunity to enter a single bid for the entire property—lock, stock, and wine barrel. That means everything—from the 1950s cars in the carriage house to the forks and knives in the butler's pantry—and everything in that cellar."

"Ann, you can't tell anyone about this."

"What? Of course I can. I have to. You must know I have a fiduciary duty to the heirs. Surely, you're not thinking I would let you, or anyone else, use this information to your benefit as a bidder."

Lord Deed Millhouse stared at the object in his hand while using that time to think. Thinking on his feet was something he was good at. The 750ml bottle was just one of thousands that had been forgotten, hidden from sight for more than fifty years. The one he was holding was more than sixty years old but in perfect condition. He had to have it—he had to have all of them! He couldn't let this silly woman spoil this for him.

Ann's admonishment burned in his head. He thought to himself, *You dumb, beautiful, sexy wench. What am I going to have to do to keep your lovely mouth shut?*

He looked into Ann's questioning eyes. "Look, Ann, I'm not interested in making money out of this. But, before you tell anyone about it, we need more input from wine experts. These wines have to be authenticated. If this is the real thing, then your find doesn't belong in just anyone's hands. What you are dealing with is irreplaceable. In that sense, the wines aren't just rare—they are priceless. I'm pretty sure most of these vintages no longer exist except in this secret cellar. When they are gone, they will be gone *forever*. If they are the real thing, they belong in the hands of collectors."

"I don't understand. Why would you think they aren't what they appear to be?"

"They are almost too good to be real! I mean, look at this label."

"What's wrong with it?"

"Nothing—that's the point! It's in almost perfect condition. You don't find wine labels this old in such good condition. It wasn't very long ago that people lost millions to a counterfeit wine scheme. So the people who would pay top dollar aren't going to take your collection at face value. They will demand proof of authenticity. If you announce the discovery before we have that proof, the experts are going to run the other way. You'll have to overcome all the negative publicity. Let's get our ducks in a row before you go public.

"Another thing, even after we have authenticated them, you need to understand that these wines are like a first-edition book. If the reader doesn't know what he has in his hands, then, to him, it is just a musty old book. But to a book lover, it has extraordinary value. You need to know who the potential buyers for these wines are—the people who collect rare wines and have the required means."

"Deed, I am so glad I called you. I hadn't thought of any of those things. Everything you said makes perfect sense."

"Good, then give me some time. Let me help you line things up before you start telling people about this. They will have all kinds of questions, and you won't have the answers. Right now, you don't even know the right questions, much less the answers."

"Okay, and for what it's worth, I'm sorry for questioning your motives."

"Of course. Ann, this is truly an important discovery. You not only have a duty to Taylor's heirs, you have an obligation to make sure it is properly regarded as the extraordinary find that it is."

"Do you have any idea about the value?"

"What I'm holding in my hands is a 1949 bottle of *Mouton Rothschild* from the *Bordeaux Pauillac Haut-Medoc* region. At Sotheby's, it would probably command five-to-six thousand dollars. There are *thousands* of first-growth wines in your cellar. Some older and worth even more! I saw cases of 1945, 1946, and 1947 vintages of wines like *Petrus, Cheval Blanc,* and *Latour.* Frankly, that might be a problem. If you put all your wine on the market at once, it will depress the market. If I were one of the heirs, I might not want the world to know just how much of this stuff we have."

"Deed, you know so much about wines; can't you give me ballpark value now?"

"If it is handled correctly, we are talking *millions.* Chinese billionaires are going to go nuts over these antique wines. Whoever owned this old place was an investor. That cellar wasn't just his for enjoyment. Some people invest in gold or art. By Jove, this guy was into wines! My guess is that cellar has twenty to twenty-five thousand bottles in it. Done right, you are talking about something in the range of twenty-five to fifty million dollars worth of wines."

"Okay, I get it. What's next?"

"We need a complete inventory, and it needs to be done by someone who knows wines."

Like everyone else with an impeccable British accent, Deed sounded knowledgeable on almost every subject. Wine was no exception. His accent alone was enough to make him an expert in Ann's mind. "Can't you do it? Maybe we could stay and work on this tonight?" she asked.

"Yes, I could, but it's going to take a while. It may be an all-nighter."

"Oh, hell, I can't—not right now."

"Why not? What could be more important?"

"It's my bodyguard."

Ann's answer set off alarm bells in Deed's head. "Why in the world do you need a bodyguard?"

"It's a long story—let's save it for later."

He was thinking fast—"You could give me a key code to the gate and let me work on the inventory tonight."

"No, it wouldn't be right. I need to be here or have someone from the firm stay with you."

He didn't want to raise suspicion. "You know, Ann, taking a night to develop a plan is probably best, anyway. Just promise me you will not do anything or tell anyone until I have a chance to check out something tonight. We can talk tomorrow morning."

"Agreed."

"Good. I'll get with you first thing tomorrow."

Deed turned his back and a smile broke out on his face. He flipped the key to his car a few inches in the air and caught it as it came back down, in silent celebration. "I've finally got my finger on the brass ring," he whispered to himself. "There's no way I'm going to let it escape!"

Ann walked back into the house to wait for her bodyguard.

— ⨍ —

Agent Sparrow drove up to the gate and pressed the old button that rang a bell inside the house announcing the arrival of a visitor.

Ann Sims looked out the French doors of the second floor where the old man used to sit daily. She pushed the speaker button next to the door. "Can I help you?"

"Yes, I'm Agent Sparrow. Are you Ann Sims?"

The question *Are you Ann Sims?* coming from the authoritative voice of the agent sounded like a challenge. Had she opened a Pandora's box? Talking to Mark Rollins might have been a mistake. She wished she could just say no, but she couldn't. "Yes, I'm Ann Sims."

"Well, I'm the cavalry. Let me in and I'll circle the wagons and keep you safe."

This time there was a disarming smile, a friendliness, in the agent's voice. Ann thought to herself, *Maybe it will be okay.* She pushed the button, the gate opened, and Sparrow drove her Dodge Durango up to the Taylor mansion.

Chapter 19

Heathcliff

By the time I had finished with Eugene, it was almost 3:00 p.m. I called Tony as I left the bar to let him know I was ready to leave the hotel. He was waiting with the car as I walked out of the Magnolia Lobby. There was still time to catch Chief Morgan and find out about the Metro police car at Sims's place. I called from Black Beauty's backseat. It took about five minutes to get through four layers of gatekeepers before I finally got to the chief.

"Mr. Rollins, I understand you are calling about Officer Purdue. What is your interest in this matter? Are you a lawyer?"

"Chief, it's Mark Rollins. You and I have worked together before."

There was a pause and then a drawn out, "Ooooh, yes! The Rainmaker affair—isn't that what you called it? How could I forget? I hope you're not planning to burn down any more houses in my jurisdiction."

"I hoped you wouldn't remember that part of our working together. You have to admit my plan to fly that plane into the Forte's house worked out in the long run. We saved their lives, and in the end, the bad guys received justice."

"Maybe so . . . but next time, please give us a call first. You know, we *are* the police, and you are *not.*"

"Point well taken. Regarding Officer Purdue, apparently you have requested that Metro keep an eye on Ms. Sims's condo. She's the woman whose dog Officer Purdue ran down. I'm calling for two reasons. First, Ms. Sims asked me to follow up regarding the incident with her dog. She wants to make sure the officer is disciplined. Second, given the arrival of the black-and-white, it doesn't take a lot of imagination to know that you must be concerned for her safety."

"You can let Ms. Sims know that Butch Purdue is no longer employed by the Belle Meade police department. After reviewing the accident reports, hearing from the citizen witnesses, and reviewing the limited video footage of post-event activity, I determined that Mr. Purdue did not conduct himself according to the professional standard we expect from members of our force."

"In other words, you fired him."

"Right."

"And I take it he blames it all on Ms. Sims."

"Among others. Mark, I don't really think that Purdue poses a threat to Sims or anyone who might have filed a complaint about the dog incident, but he was hotheaded when he left my office. I thought it wise to keep an eye on her until the man had a night to sleep on it. I was more concerned about a possible cussing-out than anything more serious. I'm just being prudent."

"Right." I had followed Chief Morgan's work for several years. I didn't buy his explanation completely. You don't waste favors between police chiefs over a few four-letter words. It was clear, however, that I wasn't going to get any more out of Chief Morgan. "Chief, I'm not going to continue to press you on this subject, but I will ask you to call me if anything develops to increase your concern over my client's safety."

"Why should I do that? This is the kind of thing we handle within the department, and we really don't need—or want—civilian involvement."

"Well, Chief, don't take it personally, but if you don't, I might mention to some of my friends over at the *Tennessean* that you had a rogue officer who ran down man's best friend. May not be front-page news, but—"

Morgan interrupted, "Okay, Mark, you win. We will keep you posted."

I called Sam Littleton and updated him regarding my conversation with Morgan. Consistent with my earlier decision, we agreed that there was no reason for the FBI to duplicate Morgan's surveillance team. We would reassess the situation later.

As I disconnected my call, we passed the Brentwood exit off of I-65.

"Tony, did you remember that we were going to stop at the WH Club before heading home?"

"Sure thing, Mr. R. According to the navigation screen there is an accident at Old Hickory and Franklin Road.

I'm going to get off at Concord and backtrack. I'll have you there in five."

— ƒ —

The Women's Health Club is in a secure building. As far as the clientele are concerned, the security is for their protection. Kidnapping for ransom is slowly making its way across the Mexican border to the States. While it hasn't reached the Nashville area, our ladies are world travelers. They think internationally. That makes them sensitive to the growing risk the wealthy face all over the globe. They also are addicted to bling—even in workout clothes, our ladies wear their diamonds. The obvious need to protect our clients and their property provides a perfect cover for the security regime that also shields our clandestine operations and the sophisticated electronics tucked out of club members' sight.

Tony let me out of the Lexus at the employee entrance in the back of the building. I waved to the monitoring camera as I inserted my keycard and entered the building. Shannon, our receptionist, was one of the people on the other end of the monitoring circuits so she was waiting for me as I walked toward the front of the building where my office is located.

"Good afternoon, Mr. Rollins. It is a fine day, isn't it?"

"Yes, it is—but I can tell that something other than that has you smiling. Out with it, Shannon."

"Well, yes, I am raising money for the earthquake victims in Haiti."

"Yes, those poor people are in dire straits. Sarah and I have already made a substantial donation to the Red Cross. What are you going to do with the money you raise? I hope you are collecting for one of the vetted organizations on the ground in Haiti."

"The Red Cross—that's my point, Mr. Rollins. Everyone is focusing on the *people*. People can usually take care of themselves. But what about the animals? Who is helping them? That is what a group of us is doing."

"What group is that, Shannon?"

"It's my church, but we are working in conjunction with ARCH, the Animal Relief Coalition for Haiti. It's a joint effort among a lot of animal organizations, including the World Society for the Protection of Animals, the WSPA. And they are working with IFAW, the International Fund for Animal Welfare and with Antigua and Barbuda Humane Societies. There are more groups joining in the effort every day. Even PETA has people on the ground. It's really a nice thing, Mr. Rollins."

"Shannon, I'm glad to hear that you are working with ARCH. I was concerned that you might be trying to do something on your own."

"Well, I wanted to do *something*, and my pastor told me about ARCH. But I did make these red and blue ribbons myself. Those are the colors of their flag. Do you know why?"

"Isn't it a knock-off of the French flag?"

"No, Mr. Rollins! The blue is to show their connection to Africa."

"That's interesting, Shannon. You know, I've always wondered why the color blue is so connected to Africa.

I suppose it has something to do with the Blue Nile. Did you know that archaeologists have discovered that blue is the predominant color of beads they uncover throughout Africa in their search for ancient artifacts?"

"Gee, I didn't know that. Well, that's why half their flag is blue. Haiti was populated by slaves from Africa—most of them from Cameroon. And the red half of the flag is supposed to represent the multiracial makeup of Haiti's population."

"The ribbon is a good idea, Shannon."

"Will you wear it for me to let people know you support our efforts to help the animals?"

"Sure. Pin it on for me, and I'll write you a check. I wouldn't want the animals of Haiti to go without."

"Mr. Rollins! It is not nice of you to make fun of me!"

"Just kidding, Shannon. I'm sure the need is real. It's just so like you to worry about the forgotten. As you said, I sent the Red Cross a big check and never even thought about the pets and livestock. But I *am* glad you are working with reputable organizations. ARCH will put qualified veterinarians on the ground. You are doing a good thing, and you are doing it right—right things right. That is important."

I headed for my office leaving Shannon with my check in her hand and a big smile on her face.

So far I had involved Bryan and his team in the Ann Sims matter, but that was pretty much it. Mariko was busy with the self-defense classes Meg assigned to her. She is teaching some of the classes, but we are also tapping resources outside of the WH Club. The ladies are taking lessons from the folks at the Uselton Arms Shooting Sports in Franklin and from several independent martial arts experts. I decided to continue to leave Mariko out of the loop, except for being on call, until it was time to take over from the FBI.

My snail-mailbox was overflowing, but it was all political. Everyone wants money. And the more you give the candidates running for office, the more they want. I made short work of the stack of mail, sending most of them unopened to the round file.

My e-mail inbox was far more interesting. Agent Sparrow had sent a short message letting me know that she had made contact with Ann Sims and that Sims had agreed to have Sparrow move into her spare bedroom for now. I liked Sparrow. She was actually DEA, so I wasn't sure how Littleton managed to get her assigned to the Sims detail. But having dealt with her before, especially during my little unpleasantness in Guatemala a couple of years back, I was happy with Littleton's choice.

I called Bryan's extension.

"I see you are in the building, Chief."

"Yes, any luck finding our missing husband?"

"Yes and no. You did say that this Paul Walton was a professor of English literature, right?"

"Right."

"Well, we hacked the registration records of Nashville motels and found that a 'Heathcliff' was registered at the Microtel Inn in the Bellevue area—close to the I-40 exit to Highway 70. And surprise, surprise, Heathcliff's first name on the registration was Paul. We contacted the front desk, and yes, Mr. Heathcliff was a motorcyclist. However, we're a day late; he checked out yesterday."

"Have we got a make on the motorcycle?"

"No, but our guess is that he is headed home. I have some people watching his place just in case."

"You may be right, but he could have moved to another hotel. Keep looking for the cycle, especially at the airport and other area hotels. If you find it, let's put a tracking device on it. Any progress regarding our rogue policeman, Butch Purdue?"

"Yes. He comes from good German stock. Full name is Conrad Otto Purdue Jr. Initials C. O. P.—how is that for irony? The nickname Butch is a German tradition. The senior usually goes by his first name, Conrad, and junior gets the handle 'Butch.' "

"Interesting. But what I want to know is where he is at all times and what he is up to."

"We will get to work on that. It would be easy if he had a cell phone we could identify, but that was part of his Belle Meade-issued supplies that he had to give up. What we'll have to do is start tracking the new numbers issued by Verizon, AT&T, and others. Once we have him in our sights, we can lock on his phone and track his movement in real time."

"Bryan, as the captain used to say to his second, 'Make it so.' We need to keep a close eye on him. I talked to Chief Morgan. He downplayed any danger to Sims but is clearly concerned that Purdue may try to confront her. We need to keep Mariko on standby just in case."

"I talked to her. She is on call—willing and ready to intercept."

"Thanks. I'm going home. Tomorrow I will be in DC, but if anything comes up, you know how to reach me."

"Don't worry, Chief, we have your back, and Meg has everything at the club under control."

"Meg is good, but even she can't control the weather, and the reports aren't looking that good. The weather people are talking about some pretty serious stuff headed our way, so make sure everyone stays alert. Just to be safe, ask Meg to review the weather emergency protocol with the staff."

"Roger that."

CHAPTER 20

Mariko Lee, WHC VP of Security

On my way out of the building, I ran into Catwoman. It was, of course, Mariko Lee, my exhibitionist vice president of security.

Mariko posed for me. "You like it, Boss?"

"I recognize it—you are Lee Meriwether as the 1966 Catwoman."

"You're no fun, Boss. You know too much!"

"I know this—I'm thankful you didn't go for Halle Berry's interpretation."

"Oh, but I would have liked to!"

"I'm sure you would have, so what constrained you? Surely, it wasn't your modesty!"

"With Halle's outfit, I wouldn't have had any place for my Beretta or my Springfield. Halle's outfit was too much skin and too much mask even for me."

"Why do you need the hardware? All Catwoman needed was her whip."

"The whip is just for show, Boss."

"I assume your outfit has something to do with teaching the ladies the art of self-defense."

"You got it, Boss—keeps things interesting."

I had been walking toward the employee entrance in the rear of the building, and Mariko was walking beside me. We had stopped to continue our conversation under the skylight where the south annex's central corridor widens to serve as a lounge area. The employee entrance door in front of us opened and in walked a curvy Latina woman. She smiled and waved when she saw Mariko. Mariko waved back and said, "Carmen, I want you to meet the boss."

The lady joined us under the skylight. "So this is the man I have heard so much about?" She held out her hand. "Mr. Rollins, I'm your new Zumba instructor, Carmen Maria Diaz."

"Carmen, it is a pleasure to meet you. You have a nice strong handshake."

"I would like to stay and talk, but right now I have a full class of ladies ready to Zumba and their instructor is almost late. The traffic was terrible. Must be the recession." She laughed and started walking away from us.

I turned to Mariko. "Well, she doesn't look like our standard-issue WH Club instructor. Carmen Maria has curves, lots of them."

"Boss, the rest of us have curves too!"

"You know what I mean. You guys are the tight, firm, low-body-fat versions. Carmen Maria Diaz doesn't exactly fit that mold, now, does she?"

"Okay, but she is Latina—hot blooded with *mucho* rhythm and that makes her a fantastic Zumba instructor."

"Zumba, Zumba, Zumba! It *is* a catchy name; I'll give you that. I must be out of the loop because I don't remember Meg mentioning it. What is it and when did we start Zumba-ing?"

"It's the new craze, Boss. It's salsa dance combined with hip-hop—big Latino influence. You know we are always changing things to keep it interesting. You have to keep up. First we had dance aerobics—jazzercise with Twiggy-like instructors. The best instructors were wannabe dancers. There was a problem, however. Jazzercise was too one-size-fits-all, so we added high/low aerobics. Then later, step, spinning, and kickboxing caught on. Dance suffered from its own popularity and more or less went out of style—kind of like disco back in the day.

"That's when the Jennifer Lopez types started showing up in movies and TV. The Latina look and their dances were glamorized—that helped usher in Zumba. You talked about curves. Well, Boss, Zumba is all about curves and hips and nice rear ends. Where jazzercise was all white bread, Zumba is spicy. It fuses hypnotic Latin rhythms and some hip-hop with pretty easy-to-follow moves. It is *exciting*. It's exhilarating. Those aren't things you usually associate with exercise.

"Meg says she would never teach Zumba. She said she would look stupid because she is about control, technique, and power. Zumba is just the opposite. It is loose. It is free form, rhythmic movement. The instructors don't look like Meg either. The best instructors are full-figured Latinas or blacks; and instead of your usual workout outfits, our Zumba clients are wearing low-rise tights and midriffs."

"I get it, Mariko. The growing Latino population is shifting our culture. What about Pilates and yoga?"

"Pilates and yoga along with body sculpting classes are always popular. Women will never give those up even when they, like our clients, can afford surgery as a short-cut. But Pilates and yoga are not cardio-fitness exercises. Looking good is at the top of our ladies' priority lists, but living to enjoy it is still important to them."

I looked at my watch. "Thanks for the update, Mariko, but I need to Zumba on out of here."

"Please!" Mariko shook her head and grimaced at the bad joke. She gave me a "you are dismissed" wave and retreated into the heart of the club.

I left the building, and Tony was waiting for me with the motor running.

"Ready to go home, Mr. R?"

"Yes, Tony. Let's do it."

"Mr. R, did you see Mariko's new wheels?"

"No, what did she get this time?"

"It's another bike."

"What happened to the Black Max?"

"Not sure. Maybe she traded it in. The new one is another little black number, however."

Tony had been using the rear passenger computer system and the display was still showing the website he last visited so I just couldn't help myself. "Tony, my man, if you are talking bike, black, and Mariko's money, then you must be talking about 'The Lady in Black.' "

"Mr. R, you always surprise me. You know your machines. I had to look it up. But you are right on target. 'The

Lady in Black' is the nickname for an F4 CC from MV Agusta designed by Claudio Castiglioni himself."

I quickly scanned the promotional text on the display. "If I remember correctly, Tony, that machine is priced at around 120 thousand dollars. The CC in the model number stands for Claudio Castiglioni, the managing director of the Italian company. He pulled out all the stops to design the model carrying his initials although their production is limited to one hundred."

"It is quite a bike." Tony's admiration could be heard in his voice.

"Mariko is quite a woman."

"You got that right, Mr. R. But then you aren't so bad yourself. I'll never understand how you stuff so much knowledge about everything into your 'little gray cells,' as you call them."

"I wasn't the first to call them the little gray cells, Tony. That was Poirot, Agatha Christie's famous detective."

"See, that's what I mean, Mr. R. You can't be stumped. You know too much!"

I smiled to myself as I quietly changed the display from "The Lady in Black" to Google.

CHAPTER 21

Billy, Drinking Partner

Ann reluctantly installed Agent Sparrow in her guestroom. Sharing her condo with another woman was uncomfortable for her—especially a woman who carried a gun. As the evening wore on, Ann retreated to the privacy of her bedroom. It had been a long day. She was still having second thoughts about this bodyguard thing. She turned on her small TV and reduced the volume to the point where she could still hear it but was pretty sure the sound didn't carry beyond her closed door. She settled into bed. She often slept with the TV on. The late-night news was broadcasting, and the weatherman was talking about the front headed toward Nashville. The chance for rain was 100 percent, heavy at times, with severe weather likely.

Ann's phone rang and she answered quickly, hoping the agent wouldn't hear it. "Hello?"

A man's angry voice assaulted her. "Are you still going through with this divorce?"

"You know I am."

"I'm not going to let you walk away from our marriage without there being something in it for me."

"Paul, our marriage has been over for a long time. You know that. And you have to stop spying on me."

"You are valuable property. I have to safeguard my investment."

"I'm not your property. That's what ended our marriage. You acted as if you owned me. You don't. You didn't then, and you certainly don't now."

"Look! I saw you with that dude all decked out in his fancy suit. And yeah, my first reaction was that I didn't like the looks of him, and I didn't like the idea of you being with him. However, I'm cool about it now. I got that out of my system. I don't give a shit anymore! You got that? I don't give a damn who you sleep with anymore."

"I assume you mean Lord Millhouse. For your information, I'm not sleeping with him—not that it is *any* of your business."

"Oh, but you *are* my business! And it's time for my investment to pay off."

"What are you talking about?"

"You can have your damn divorce, but I want a piece of the action. Don't forget I know your little secret."

"Paul, you're too late. There isn't going to be any money."

"Huh?"

"I decided I can't live with this anymore."

"Oh, come on. You're not the suicidal type."

"You're an idiot. You've always been pretty stupid for a college professor. I'm not talking about killing myself.

What I did wasn't right, and I've decided I can't keep the money anymore. I can do just fine on my own."

"What the hell are you planning to do?"

"I'm meeting with Uncle Eugene later this week, and I'm going to tell him everything."

"Don't be crazy. You're telling me you're going to walk away from more than sixty million dollars, just like that? We were together too long for me to believe that."

"You don't know me as well as you think you do. That is *exactly* what I'm going to do."

"If you really mean that—and I don't believe it for a minute—then you're stupid. I'm telling you now that, even if you are really willing to walk away from all that money, I am not. I am *not* walking away—*period.*"

"You don't have any say in it. My mind is made up."

"Oh, but you're wrong; I want my share of the action. I called to tell you I want ten million dollars, then I'll get out of your life forever."

"Well, you aren't going to receive a nickel."

"We'll see about that! You can't buffalo me." The line went dead.

Ann lay staring at the ceiling as she rehashed the phone call in her head. *Should I tell Agent Sparrow about it? What does Paul think he could do to make me change my plans to settle things with Eugene?*

She finally decided there was nothing he could do—no need to tell Sparrow—and fell asleep.

— ʃ —

It was 1:30 in the morning. The bar would be closing in another thirty minutes. But Eugene and his new friend weren't ready to call it a night. At least, they weren't ready to go their separate ways. His friend was quite good looking—long blond hair, shorter and much younger than Eugene. He had a well-built athletic body. It wasn't the body of some dumb jock. His was more like that of a dancer or a runner. He said he was in Music City looking for work, and he looked the part—Western boots, tight blue jeans that showed off his assets, fitted shirt, and a black cowboy hat. At first Eugene thought he might be in one of the country bands playing around the hotel. But his new friend explained he had heard so much about the hotel that he had decided to check out the place.

Eugene bought him a beer, then another and another, and then a barbeque dinner and more beer. Eugene suggested they go up to his room. He had a bottle of Gentleman Jack in his room and some movies they could watch. Billy smiled and thought that was a good idea so the two left the bar together. Eugene gave Billy's cute butt a pat as they exited Rusty's Sports Bar & Grill.

Neither Eugene nor his new friend noticed the man sitting alone near the door as they left. The man waited until the couple was a good twenty steps away, and then he followed.

Billy often worked the bars around Nashville. Before the night was over, he would have his target's billfold, and the target would be headed toward the biggest hangover ever. He already had the steps planned out—choreographed. He would offer to pour the Jack Daniels whiskey, and Eugene wouldn't remember anything after that.

The third man followed the couple. At the last minute, he entered the same elevator and punched the button to the floor above the one Eugene had pushed. When they got off, he hung back. But just as the door was closing, he pushed the Open Door button and got off on the same floor. The couple had already started down the hall to Eugene's room. The stranger watched as Eugene tacked his way, zigzagging, down the hall with his young puppy in tow. After several failed attempts to unlock and enter his hotel room, Eugene handed the keycard to the younger man, who succeeded on his first try.

It was almost 2:00 a.m. The hall was empty and silent. The stranger figured if the young guy was a pro, he would be out of Eugene's room in thirty minutes tops. He spoke out loud to himself, "I would take a bet on twenty."

The time passed slowly. It was beginning to look as if whatever plan he had for Eugene would have to wait for another time and another place. But his time hadn't been wasted; he had learned something important. He had learned how easy it would be to lure Eugene Sims to his death. He was not only gay; he was on the prowl.

Just as the stranger was about to abandon his watchful post, he heard the door opening. He turned away and started walking down the hall in the opposite direction. He heard the door close. The stranger continued his walk as if returning to his own room. When he heard the elevator stop on the floor, the stranger turned in time to see Eugene's young friend entering the elevator, at the same time tossing something into the trash container next to the elevator door.

The stranger retraced his steps, removed the top of the shiny brass trash receptacle and saw a wallet just as he expected. He carefully used his handkerchief to retrieve the wallet. Any money that had been there was gone. Credit cards, pictures, driver's license—and the keycard to Eugene's room were still there, however.

The man put the billfold and card in his jacket pocket and removed surgical gloves from another pocket. He turned and walked to Eugene's room, checked up and down the hall, and then put on the gloves and softly knocked. No one answered. He inserted the card into the door lock. The green light came on. He turned the handle slowly, looked up and down the hall again, and quickly entered the room.

Eugene was face down on the floor. The man checked for a pulse. Eugene was alive but unresponsive. The young man had obviously drugged him. Perfect, the stranger thought. Sims and his companion had been in the bar for hours. A lot of people had seen the couple. The companion probably had his prints on the wallet and all over the room.

The stranger turned Eugene's unconscious body over so that he was lying on his back. He knew just where to place his hands and gently press—firm enough to stop the flow of oxygen but gently enough to avoid bruising. It was easy when the victim was unable to resist. Killing with your hands in a fight leaves marks, but when the victim can't fight back, you can do it without leaving a trace. Eugene slowly died without a struggle, never aware that he was being murdered.

The killer gave a chuckle as he examined his handi-work and whispered into the dead man's ear. "Eugene, my friend, this was almost *too* easy. The authorities are going to pin this on your man-whore. Even *he* will think he did it! Everyone will think your lover and whatever drug he dosed you with were the culprits."

Eugene's real killer returned the room keycard to the billfold after wiping both to remove fingerprints. He slow-ly opened the door, checked the hall in both directions, and quietly left the room. Before he got on the elevator, he knocked over the trash receptacle and then threw the billfold into the spilled trash. He wanted to make sure it would be found.

CHAPTER 22

DC

The weather people were still talking about heavy rains headed our way as Tony drove me to the airport. I thought that was unusual. Weather forecasting is still not an exact science. Short of a hurricane, meteorologists don't usually forecast with such certainty, and certainly not as far in advance as they had been doing this time. Nashville is one of those places where people say that if you don't like the weather, just wait awhile. So what was the big deal? Why the long advance warning? I looked out the car window, and things did look pretty lousy. It was not raining, but there were certainly some dark, mean-looking clouds building on the horizon. Luckily, I was flying north and a little east, away from those clouds.

Tony delivered me planeside by 8:00 a.m., and we were off the ground heading for DC by 8:15.

— ƒ —

The slick private jet dropped quickly once in the DC airspace and flew low over the Potomac River on its approach to Reagan International. Once on the ground, we taxied to the general aviation terminal. Looking out the plane's window, I saw a black-suited driver standing by the rear passenger door of a shiny black Town Car. He watched our approach as we taxied up to the Signature Flight Support facility. Signore Greco's team was as efficient as usual. The pilot cut the engines. The copilot opened the plane's door and lowered the built-in stairs.

While I was taking care of my business in the city, the pilots would be taking care of theirs. The plane would be refueled, cleaned, and ready to fly as soon as I returned. General aviation facilities like Signature are called FBOs, Fixed-Base Operators, and Signature competes for traffic with the twenty-one other area airports and FBOs in the DC area. They do that by catering to the pilots, not the passengers. Signature's pilot lounge is first class; thus, they are the preferred FBO in the area.

The driver met me as I stepped onto the tarmac. "Mr. Rollins, my name is Jack House, your driver today."

The customary uniform for drivers is a dark suit, usually black, a solid-color tie, white shirt, and chauffer's hat. Jack House was not standard. He wore the black suit all right, but underneath he had on a tight black T-shirt instead of the customary white dress shirt. There was no hat and his head was clean-shaven.

As he and I walked from the plane to his car, he explained that Greco's limo service in the DC area used only drivers trained in personal defense. In Jack's case, he was a seventh-degree black belt and a certified instructor in the art of Kung Fu San Soo. He also pulled back his coat to show me the PX4 Beretta Storm, a 9mm sub-compact, which he wore in a hi-ride mini belt holster. His show-and-tell was designed to put me, his passenger, at ease. I asked why firepower and martial art skills were needed. Jack was quick to explain. His customers came from all over the world—a good percentage from Mexico, South America, and the Middle East. As Jack explained, in their home countries, these men didn't go anywhere without security, so they expect it when they come to the States.

He opened the door for me. "I have some people from Europe who think America is the Wild West. They read about guns and murders here. Mr. Rollins, did you know that you are more likely to be murdered in DC than any-where else in the country other than Detroit?"

I didn't answer. He really wasn't expecting an answer and I knew it.

In the 1990s, a civilian in DC was three times more likely to be killed than a member of our military. That was when the city got its nickname as the "murder capital of the US." It's better today, largely because there are 25 percent fewer people living in the District. The DC mur-der rate of more than 30 per 100,000 population is still one of the highest in the nation. Jack was right, but only if you are African American. The sad fact is that almost all the homicides in the DC area are the result of blacks killing blacks. If you're white, the homicide-per-thousand statistic doesn't apply to you.

I looked down to be sure I was wearing my lapel flag pin. I was. And it was upside down, as it should be to signal distress. I mean, this is the seat of our national government. If we have a national government unable to manage its home base, foster a business environment that provides its people, of all colors and ethnic backgrounds, with decent jobs rather than welfare checks, and provide a safe, secure place to live, how can we depend on that government to perform its greater national job? It is failing us on all counts today.

The bums, all of them, need to be tossed out of office, and the District turned over to Disneyland. Disneyland took New York's Broadway back from the pimps and drug pushers. They can turn the District into the clean, safe tourist park it needs to be. While we are at it, let's turn the southern border over to Bank of America. We can make border crossers legal without making them citizens:

> *Want to come across our southern border? Just step up to a Bank of America ATM that instantly takes your fingerprints, collects a little DNA, records an image of your iris, checks criminal records here and in your home country, and then prints out a combination temporary worker's permit and credit card with your picture on it—all within minutes.*

If you carry the card and do no wrong, you are a legal immigrant. Get caught without the card, or commit a crime, and you are out of here. It seems simple enough to me.

Jack, the driver, was a pro. It takes one to navigate the maze of streets now blocked off for security around the Capitol. When he let me out at the Capitol Hill Club, I found my lunch partners waiting for me in the lobby.

CHAPTER 23

Throwdown

Ann closed the door to her office after Agent Sparrow and she arrived in the morning. She wanted to avoid any more questions than necessary about her unusual guest. Luckily, her office was not an associate's cubbyhole. She was a partner—the youngest and most recent—but still a partner.

When her mentor, John Gray Hanger, had retired a few months ago, the partners assigned his 25 x 20–foot office to Sims. The desk she inherited was masculine—dark mahogany—and sat in front of a matching credenza. Her desk chair was equally masculine, but at least it wasn't black. Her predecessor had avoided the usual black and opted instead for dark blood-red leather with mahogany arms. The three guest chairs arranged in front of her desk were the same combination of mahogany wood and blood-colored leather with antique brass tacking. Placed against a wall with no windows, the deep-cushioned, cream-color sofa added a little bit of light to the room.

An English tea table in front of the sofa held copies of the morning newspapers—*U.S. News and World Report*, the *Wall Street Journal*, and the *Tennessean*.

Agent Sparrow was seated on the sofa dressed as usual in her navy blazer, gray slacks, and simple black pumps. Her strawberry blond hair was cut short. Her nails were manicured, but the polish was clear. If she was wearing makeup, it was very light. She was an attractive, athletic woman—five feet ten inches tall without shoes. Hidden from sight by her blazer, belted on her right side she carried the standard issue .40 S&W Heckler & Koch-USP weapon in a Blackhawk Close Quarters Carbon Fiber Holster with a Serpa release. Utilitarian in appearance, the holster is built for draw speed not looks, and it is often hailed as the fastest drawing holster on the market.

Ann Sims was reviewing drafts of the Auction Agreement as well as all the bidder registration documents, including the bidder consent forms detailing "terms and conditions of business," as they are called in the trade.

Per the Agreement, the Taylor property was first to be auctioned as a whole because the heirs wanted it over with as quickly as possible. If the hammer price met the confidential minimum set by the heirs, then it would be over and the bidder takes all. If the bids should fail to meet the minimum, the auctioneer would begin auctioning off individual lots of personal property items with the final item being the real estate itself. That was Ann's problem. If Lord Millhouse was right, the wine no one else knew about was worth more than the property itself. At a minimum, it should be excluded from the current auction and handled by specialty auctioneers who cater to collectors. She needed to reach a decision while there was still an opportunity to negotiate a change in the agreement, and time was running out.

There was a commotion in the hall. Sparrow quickly looked up from the paper she was reading. The door flew open and an angry, red-faced John Randall burst into the office. He was screaming and rushing toward Ann.

"You lousy bitch! I want to kill you! You two-bit—"

Sparrow sprang off the sofa, drawing her weapon and moving to obstruct the intruder—all in what seemed like one fluid movement.

Randall didn't finish his tirade. Sparrow, her weapon forward in both hands, used her right leg and Randall's forward motion to sweep his legs out from under him. He nosedived forward, arms outstretched to break his fall. Sparrow was on top of him, her knee in his back, and the gun in her right hand against his neck. With her left hand, she reached behind her back and released the restraints, handcuffs.

Randall screamed, "What the hell!? Who are you? Get the fuck off me!"

With her left hand, she reached across and slammed the cuff on Randall's right wrist, yanking his arm behind his back. She holstered her weapon, pulled Randall's left arm behind his back, and cuffed his two wrists together. Sparrow looked up for the first time and her eyes encountered a shocked and bewildered Ann Sims. Sparrow, her adrenaline still flowing at tiger-attack levels, ignored Randall's rants, and commanded, "Call 911."

Randall was crying and shouting, "Call the police! Help me, for God's sake! Help me, someone!"

In her shock, Ann automatically reached for the phone. Then she pulled her hand back and shouted at the agent, "No! Get off him! He works here!"

Sparrow got to her feet. Then she literally lifted Randall off the floor with one hand on his belt and the other on the back of his shirt. She slammed him into one of the side chairs as she sternly repeated her command, "Call 911; *do it now*."

"Take those cuffs off that man. He's our firm's administrator."

"Look, Sims, I'm here because you asked for security. Now call 911."

"No. I was wrong. I don't want you here. I want you out of here—out of my office *and* my home. Now take the cuffs off him and get out!"

The agent was stunned. "Look, the man said he wanted to kill you."

Randall was beginning to think straight. "My car—my new car—some asshole keyed my new car—both sides of it."

Ann, still standing behind her desk, asked in amazement, "You think I did that?"

"There was a note—"

Agent Sparrow interrupted. "Show me the note."

"I tore it up. I was so mad, I tore it to shreds."

Ann asked, "What did it say?"

"To back off and leave the lady alone. I assumed that referred to you."

"John, that could *not* have been about me. I wouldn't have had anything to do with damaging your car."

Sparrow begrudgingly removed Randall's handcuffs.

His hands free, Randall's anger and machismo were on the rise. Seething, he stood up, rubbing his wrists. "You could have hurt me!" Looking at Sparrow, he screamed, "I am going to sue the shit out of you!"

Agent Sparrow was taking none of it. "Pop off again, and the cuffs will go back on. I'll haul your ass downtown and let you cool off in a cell."

"Who the hell *are* you?"

"I'm a federal officer assigned to protect this lady. You stormed in here saying you wanted to kill her. Seems to me you asked for what I gave you."

"Come on—that's just something people say. You can't goddamn *really* believe I intended to kill her."

"It's my job to believe you when you threaten someone. I'm going to take you at your word and stop you."

Enraged, Randall waved his hands wide and shouted to the room in general: "To hell with it—to hell with *all* of you! I am out of here. I quit!" He looked directly at Ann Sims and snarled, "Screw you and this goddamn law firm." Randall stormed out of the office. As he walked through the door, he raised his hand over his head and gave the room's occupants the "you are number one" sign with his middle finger.

Neither Sparrow nor Sims said anything for what seemed like several minutes. Then Ann spoke. "I'm sorry Agent Sparrow, but I was wrong about security. I don't want it anymore. I was probably just being paranoid anyway, but I can't have this. I can't have someone hanging around all the time ready to manhandle my coworkers or friends—or even a client, for God's sake—if they happen to say or do the wrong thing."

"Are you sure about this? Anyone would have acted the same way I did under the circumstances."

"I'm sure any security guard would have. That's why I'm so sure I don't want this anymore."

"Well, I don't take my orders from you, so I have to check in and see what the higher-ups want me to do."

"You can use my phone on the desk."

"No, thanks. It's better if I call using my cell. I'll make it out in the hall."

"You can use the office next to mine. Its owner is in court today."

Sparrow nodded and left Ann's office to make the call.

Ann numbly sat down behind her desk. She was too shaken to refocus her attention on the documents she had been reviewing.

Sparrow returned after a few minutes.

"Well, it looks like you get your wish. I really hope you are doing the right thing. The smart thing to do is to listen to your gut. You thought you were in danger and that is a pretty good reason to stick with the plan."

"No, I was wrong. This is the right thing. Thank you for your concern, but I want to go back to just being an attorney—one without a posse."

"Okay. Here's my card. If something happens, don't hesitate to call."

CHAPTER 24

The Brain Trust

Lunch had been served, eaten, and taken away. With the niceties behind us, it was time for my guests to get serious about the purpose of our meeting. Those discussions didn't need to be interrupted by phone calls, and my phone had been nagging me throughout lunch. I had ignored the first three calls. Now it was vibrating again. I knew whoever was trying to reach me wasn't going to give up until I finally took their call. This was the time to do it. I took the phone out of my pocket and glanced at the display. It was Littleton.

"I'm sorry, gentlemen, but this appears to be a call I need to take before we get down to business."

They nodded. I got up from the table and walked toward the restrooms for a little privacy as I pushed the answer button.

Littleton spoke before I could say anything, "Can you talk?"

"I'm in a business meeting. Can this wait?"

"Sorry, but I thought you would want to know that we were just fired."

"By Sims?" I asked in amazement.

"Yes. I won't go into details, but the important thing right now is that she has no one covering her back. Mark, our involvement was questionable to start with. Now that the lady has told us to take a walk, there is nothing I can do at this point."

"I understand, Sam."

"I just hope your young lady knows what she's doing." That finished our conversation.

I returned to the table. "Sorry for that interruption, gentlemen, but you now have my undivided attention. What can the WHC team and I do for you?"

The admiral picked up where he left off, "As I indicated during lunch, we have a client who lost hundreds of millions in auction rate securities, also known as ARS. ARS holdings are long-term debt instruments where the interest rate is regularly reset through a Dutch auction. After 2007, most such auctions failed. The market froze. Some investment banks that distributed auction rate securities repurchased them at par value rather than face lawsuits from clients who claimed the securities were marketed as cash equivalent funds. Not so in the case of our target bank.

"Here is the lay of the land. It is a German bank with a US arm. The bank's wealth management group was handling our client's funds. At the same time handlers at the bank were loading our client up with ARS paper, the bank was liquidating its own ARS portfolio. When the market blew up, the bank personally had zero invested in ARS holdings—no government or corporate ARS holdings. The bank had liquidated *their* entire holdings of the same stuff they were buying on behalf of our client.

"That just doesn't happen through normal trading. We're talking about billions of dollars turned over in a matter of weeks. It defies common sense that these were innocent trading moves. Someone in the bank must have seen the collapse coming—someone high up in the organization, someone whose job scope reached across both the bank's trading operation and the bank's wealth management group."

"So you are looking for evidence that the bank withheld information from your client?" I interjected.

"Mr. Rollins, it's a little more complicated than that. You see, normally there's a 'Chinese wall' between the bank's trading department and the wealth management groups. The bank's traders aren't allowed to signal its buys and sells to the wealth group.

"If the bank signaled making a major trade to the wealth management people, they could arbitrage on behalf of their client and make quick millions on insider information. So if the bank was doing business as usual, that is, if it was solely engaged in customary investment activities, it would be off the hook.

"What we are looking for is evidence that the bank knew there were structural problems with the securities—that they were 'damaged goods,' so to speak. If that were the case, then the higher-ups had a fiduciary responsibility to communicate that information to their clients being handled by the wealth group. In fact, they had a responsibility that even went beyond that. If we could find evidence of that, then even people who purchased ARS securities from others might have a claim against the bank."

"With all due respect, Admiral, the latter seems a little far-fetched to me."

"Yes, I'm not sure any lawyer would want to take such a case on a contingency basis, but we are talking about billions of dollars if someone wanted to do a Hail Mary. The bank's obligation to its wealth management clients is much clearer."

"I have to admit it's still a little fuzzy to me. There is this 'Chinese wall' thing that separates the two areas of the bank, but in certain cases, they have an obligation to breach that wall. You think a jury would grasp a line that blurry?"

"Well, Mark, you work with lawyers, right?"

"I did."

"Okay, Mark, think of it this way. The bank's obligations are not much different from a lawyer's. The lawyer has an obligation of confidentiality to his clients, but he or she is also an officer of the court. And the duty to the court trumps the confidentiality obligation in certain cases. For example, if a lawyer becomes aware of a crime about to be committed, he is required by law to breach his duty of confidentiality and take action to prevent the crime. In this case, if the bank had determined that the securities were flawed. In layman's terms, when the ARS securities did not serve their advertised purpose, then, like the lawyer and his crime, they had to disclose their findings."

"So you need a smoking gun. It really boils down to the words they used to arrive at or to communicate their decision to sell."

"Exactly. And these guys are smart enough not to use their company e-mail. So what we are looking for can be *anywhere* in cyberspace. That is where your group comes in. What is it you call them?"

"The brain trust."

"Yes, your brain trust. Find e-mails under any name on any server between or among the various parties in the bank—and then look for the right words."

"And for that, you are offering five million to be paid up front and a twenty million dollar bonus if we actually find your smoking gun?"

"That's it."

"If my team finds the smoking gun, it means the bank has been behaving badly. Given that and the money offered, it is an offer I can't refuse."

"It's settled then. I have prepared a one-page memorandum of understanding for the two of us to sign, and if you will give me the required information, we will wire the five million dollars to your bank."

The document was simple so I had no problem signing it. Bank of America had provided me with the written transfer instructions before I left Nashville and I turned those over to the admiral.

The waiter brought the check to the table while we were talking. I signed it, pushed back from the table, and rose. I was worried about Ann Sims and didn't want to spend any more time than necessary in the District. It was time to go home.

"Gentlemen, it has been a pleasure, but I know time is critical to your cause, so let me get back to Nashville and start the ball rolling."

— ✗ —

It was after 5:00 p.m. by the time we ended our negotiations, shook hands, and went our separate ways. A text message had vibrated my phone during the admiral's explanation of the issues. It was from Bryan. "This Walton guy may not be as smart as I was giving him credit. A William Darcy checked into Opryland Hotel last night. While it could be a coincidence, my guess is that this Darcy is likely to be our professor of English literature."

Leaving the Capitol Hill Club, I was surprised to be walking into mixed precipitation—rain and sleet. A cold front had passed through. The weather forecaster obviously missed it. The storm was supposed to move offshore along the Carolinas but apparently turned north. Traffic was at a standstill.

I called the pilot and heard the bad news. There was a mechanical problem with the plane's deicing equipment. The pilot had called back to Nashville for a replacement plane to deadhead to DC, but the weather shut down that plan. Not only was air traffic backed up all along the northeast, but pounding rains in Nashville were also causing problems. We were grounded until the mechanics could make the necessary repairs and the weather improved in Nashville.

CHAPTER 25

Purdue's Dilemma

Butch Purdue was determined to pay the owner of that worthless dog back for ruining his life. He had joined the Army right out of Fairview High School. He served his due in the military as a member of the U.S. Army's 101st Airborne Division. His combat experience began in 1990 when his unit, the Screaming Eagles, dropped into Kuwait and fired the first shots in the war to liberate Kuwait. In 2003, he was back in Kuwait as a member of the force preparing for the combat operation against Saddam Hussein's regime. It was the Screaming Eagles that killed Uday and Qusay Hussein.

He couldn't stop thinking about the nearly twenty years he had devoted to his country, only to be unceremoniously encouraged *not* to reenlist. He had an honorable discharge, but they made it clear he wasn't wanted back. "Reenlist and we will find charges to bring against you" was what the sergeant major and the judge advocate's buddy had said. Seems they thought he had an anger management problem.

Hell yeah, I'm angry, Purdue fumed to himself. *I've been shot at by ragheads. I've watched my buddies get blown to bits by IEDs. I picked up body parts with the stupid idea that they might be able to sew a foot or an arm back on. I watched those damn women in their damn burqas walk up to a checkpoint and blow everyone up. Then they expected me to share a bunk with stinking Muslims. Hell no, there is no place for a raghead—no place for a damn Muslim—in my fucking Army. Hell, they even let them carry their prayer rugs with them—even on deployments. That is crazy shit. What stupid political ass decided we need ragheads in the Army? Now you got to watch your back from your own men.*

I've got a drawer full of medals. I was a goddamn hero, and it meant nothing. Now it's the same with the police job. I run over a damn dog, and they kick me out. Hell, in some of the countries I've been in, they eat dogs. Over in Iraq, they think dogs are the devil. It's all because of that Rollins jerk and the Sims woman. They're the ones that made such a big deal out of this.

Purdue started thinking about the young woman driving a sporty little Mini Cooper convertible—yellow with black racing stripes—he had pulled her over on Belle Meade Boulevard. It was three in the morning and she had been partying at one of the homes in Belle Meade. He could have hauled her in. She was real scared. She wasn't like those Iraq women—no burqa for this babe. She was showing a lot of skin. And she was scared. He told her he would follow her back to her place—to make sure she got home safely. She wasn't a dummy; she knew the deal. She knew he could have put her cute little ass behind bars while she sobered up.

She lived in a condo off West End just on the other side of Murphy Road. When they got to her place, he walked her to her door all gentlemanly like. They played a little game. He told her he should go in first to make sure it was safe. She knew what he was doing. She was real thankful, too—too damn thankful. That was why he was late for the shift change and was racing to get back to the station.

Purdue shook his head and thought, *Pleasure and pain—that is the way it is. None of this would have happened if it hadn't been for that little lady in the Cooper, but she only reminds me of pleasure. Sims is all pain, however, and all because of her damn dog that shouldn't have been in the road anyway.*

I've seen pictures of Sims in the paper—not my type. Ah shit, be honest, Purdue, he said to himself, *I'm not her type. Sure I would like some of that, but I'm not likely to get any!* The thought made him angry.

He shook his head again. *I just want to tell the bitch what I think of her. Yeah, I would like to hurt her. But maybe if I could just get her to talk to Chief Morgan, I could get back on the force. I mean, shit, what am I going to do? Out of the Army and fired from the police—hell, at best I'm looking at a security job in a mall. I need back on the force. But, there is no way any police force is going to hire me if they know I got fired. I'll be nice to her. I have got to get her to talk to the chief. If she won't do it—then I'll let her have it. I won't hurt her. They would fucking hang me if I hurt her. Purdue, you have got to keep it together—keep it together, man.*

He was driving his 2004 Nissan Frontier truck. It blended in with the construction vehicles constantly around the condo complex. The Metro car he had spotted earlier hadn't paid much attention to him when he drove by. This time the black-and-white was nowhere around. He decided it was now or never. One of the condos in the row behind Sims's unit was being renovated. There were already pickup trucks and a van parked near the unit. Purdue pulled his pickup close to the others. He got out and began walking toward the back of Sims's condo. He looked like any other construction worker in his jeans and T-shirt.

The lock on the rear door appeared simple enough. Purdue pulled the small kit from his pocket and began working on the tumblers. It took him less than fifteen seconds to align the tumblers and unlock the door. He slowly opened the door and listened for the beep of an alarm system—a warning that all hell would break loose if the right code wasn't entered within seconds. There was no beep. An alarm control box was mounted on the wall next to the door he had entered. It wasn't set.

He stepped inside just as the rain started. He took a deep breath and could smell her. Even if she wasn't home, the smell of her still lingered. He moved silently, and slowly he began to realize just how stupid he was being. He had broken into her house. If she was home, what was he going to do? Hell, she would have the right to shoot him. If she screamed, what would he do? It was a bad idea. It was like a dream—being far out on a limb or ledge and no way back. He had to get out. He had to get out *now*.

But he could come back later, he knew how now. *No, No, No—you have to keep it together, man. You don't need her. You need your job back. Leave her a note. No, are you crazy? If she knew you were here ... Hell, if she just suspected you knew where she lived, she would go ballistic. There has to be a better way. Mail her an apology. Accidentally be in the same restaurant or the courthouse. Yes, the courthouse, that wouldn't frighten her. Get your head on straight, man, and get the hell out of here—I mean now!*

Still . . . maybe after I get my job back—

CHAPTER 26

Storm Warnings

With Sparrow gone, Ann had settled down enough to return to the Auctioneer Agreement but was interrupted by her phone. "Hello?"

"Hey, babe, what did you do to poor John?"

"Oh, it's too long a story for the telephone, Eli."

"Well, we are minus one administrator. He cleaned out his desk and told us where to go."

"I'm sorry about that."

"Hey, babe, he was a pipsqueak. I'm happy to see him go. Maybe we'll get someone with balls next time."

"For someone without balls, he sure never seemed to have a problem raking me over the coals anytime he felt like it."

"You're just a girl."

"Oh, that—you think?"

"Yes. I think."

"Eli, the man was raving. He was mad as hell and taking it out on me. You didn't have anything to do with that, did you?"

"Oh, my lady, pray, what doth thou mean?"

Ann found no humor in his sarcasm. "Someone keyed his car."

"It was a *Saturn*. Who drives a Saturn unless they are still in college?"

"I hope you didn't do it. I do not need a big brother."

"Surely, you don't think of me as a *brother*. We would be sinning against nature."

"Eli, you know what I mean."

"Look, babe, I'm not going to let my girl be jumped on by some puny little asshole."

"I'm not your *girl*."

"Babe, you are breaking my heart."

"That doesn't mean I don't like having you in my bed—just lay off the ownership thing. I've been there, and I don't like it."

"Okay, okay. You're a free bird—but you're *my* bird—and I get nervous when I see tomcats hanging around."

"Stop that. I swear if you don't stop, I'll change the locks to my condo. I'm *not* going to be your executive catnip." He laughed and she continued, "I don't understand why men want to put a no-trespassing sign on me. It's always that way—I don't want that. Not again, damn it!"

"Okay, babe, don't go crazy on me. I'll back off. But you are still my pretty little rich girl."

"Eli, you say the most aggravating things. If you're after my money, you are going to be out of luck—don't forget about Uncle Eugene."

"Sure, babe, but I have a feeling dear old Uncle Eugene won't be a problem."

"No, Eli, you were right from the start. You know the man is going to be pissed out of his mind. I just hope he doesn't kill me."

"Maybe and maybe not, babe."

"Well, one thing is for sure. After this week there won't be any monetary reasons for Paul to continue resisting the divorce."

"Speaking of the devil, where is that loser husband of yours?"

"I hope he's back in Atlanta. I'm afraid he'll do something stupid before the divorce is final. I don't like being alone at night right now. Can you come over tonight?"

"I thought you were mad at me."

"I am, but we could make up, and I could use the company. Oh, by the way, I have a surprise for you. But I can't give it to you yet."

"On come on, babe, don't hold back on me."

"I said it is a surprise, dummy. It's about the Taylor place, but you'll have to wait. I'll tell you later."

"I hope you haven't been nosing around the place. After all these years, it's not safe. Plus, the heirs want to turn that white elephant into money, and they don't want any complications. The auction is just days away. Concentrate on the paperwork and stay away from the place."

"You've been telling me that ever since you turned this thing over to me. Why did you dump it on me, anyway?"

"With Burroughs gone, I inherited a lot of fires that we have to put out. I'm overloaded, so I thought it was best to have someone else handle the Taylor details."

"I really need to talk to you, Eli. Can you come by to-night? Say about eight?"

"That sounds like a plan. Let's make it from eight to eight."

"Oh, I see you are expecting breakfast too."

"I think we will both be famished in the morning."

Ann giggled. "It's a date, and I'll tell you my little secret over dinner."

"I can't wait, babe—for dessert, that is."

"I have another call, Eli, so until tonight—" Ann pressed the second line button to take the incoming call. Back to her professional voice, she said, "This is Ann Sims."

"Ann, my dear, it is so nice to hear your lovely voice again. Do you want to meet me at the mansion? I think I have everything we need to decide how to handle your hot potato."

"Yes, I'm so glad you called, Deed—the sooner the better. I can leave for the Taylor place right now if that suits you."

"Wonderful. And, I trust that you have kept your little discovery a secret, just as we discussed?"

"Yes, but I can't tell you how nervous that makes me."

"Well, just another few hours and then you can do whatever you think is the right thing to do."

"Great! I can't tell you how much I appreciate your help on this. I will see you in about twenty-five minutes."

"I'm afraid it may take you a little longer than that. Have you looked outside?"

"No, why?"

"Rain—and lots of it. I don't think I have ever been in rain this heavy. It has slowed traffic down considerably, so be prepared, my dear."

"I will. Thanks for the warning."

After the call ended, Lord Millhouse sat studying the rough inventory list he had compiled from his memory. Granted it wasn't complete, but it was the best he could do for now. He would try again to convince Ann not to share this secret with the world. They could split the money and neither would ever have to work again. He played the arguments out in his mind. *We could travel. Hell, both of us could afford our own 747 for that matter. It will be damn hard for her to walk away from this gold mine. If she won't go for it, she is one stupid bitch. The smart thing to do is back a truck up to the door and haul all of it away before the auction. It would be so simple if she weren't around—if I could just make her disappear and get away with it. To be, or not to be: that is the question. I'm beginning to understand why the question was so hard for Hamlet to answer.*

— ✠ —

Before leaving for the Taylor place, Ann made a decision to tell Eli about the cellar sooner rather than later. She trusted him, and the truth is she didn't know Lord Millhouse all that well. She needed someone else besides Lord Millhouse to discuss the options with. She got the bottle she had taken from the mansion, her surprise for him, and walked to his office on the other side of the building. He wasn't there. She retraced some of her steps and stopped by his secretary's cubical. She was listening to a small radio.

With a big smile on her face, Ann asked, "Gloria, where is your boss?"

"Hello, Ms. Sims. He just left for a board meeting at the Book Company. I expect him back, but I'm not sure of the time."

"If you don't mind, I want to leave something for him in his office."

"Certainly, Ms. Sims. I will tell him to look for it."

"Thanks."

"If you are going out, be sure to take an umbrella." Pointing toward the radio, she added, "They say we are going to get *a lot* of rain before this is over."

Ann walked into Eli's office and placed the bottle on the credenza behind his desk. She sat at his desk and wrote a note, put it in an envelope, and placed it against the bottle. In the note, she told him about the secret room, the cellar, and that she planned to tell the heirs tomorrow. Then she would start the ball rolling to have the wine excluded from the current auction. She decided not to mention Lord Millhouse.

CHAPTER 27

Shots Fired

Ann and Lord Millhouse exited the mansion. They were standing next to Ann's car under the covered part of the drive. Lord Millhouse was preparing to make a run for his car parked in the rain. Ann's cell phone rang. She looked at the display. The call was from Eli. All day long she had been getting calls that she let go unanswered. They were from Rollins and others with whom she didn't want to talk, but she was always available for Eli. She answered her phone and created some space between her and a waiting Lord Millhouse.

"Eli, I guess you got the little present I left you?" The rain had seemed to intensify while they were in the house. "What? Say that again Eli? It is hard to hear you with all this rain."

This time she didn't have a problem hearing him—Eli was shouting. "Damn it, Ann! What the hell are you doing? All you were supposed to do was handle the goddamn paperwork! That's *all*—not mess around in that old house and its basement!"

"But, Eli, doesn't this change everything?"

"No, it better damn not if you want to remain a partner in this law firm. No! Even more—if you want to keep practicing law—you will forget about the wine and get on with the damn auction."

Ann was flabbergasted. She had never heard Eli like this. He was her lover not her boss—not this way. He was not someone who would ever threaten her like this. "Eli, that wine is worth more than all the rest of the property put together."

"Ann, that old place is to be sold 'as is' with everything in place. That's the way everyone wants it. That is the way the heirs want it. And dammit, they want it sold immediately! No delays, understand? Hell, the stuff in that cellar is probably mostly vinegar by now anyway. We don't need you complicating things at this late date."

Ann's own anger was building. He had no right to talk to her like this, and he was wrong! His position made no sense. Then it hit her, and her anger exploded. "Eli, you knew about the secret cellar, didn't you?"

There was silence on the other end of the phone. That silence told her all she needed to know.

"Eli, you asshole, you were going to bid, weren't you?" Ann was shouting into the phone. She noticed Millhouse moving closer to her. She turned her back to him and made an effort to lower her voice. "That's why you recused yourself! Isn't it? Admit it!"

"Ann, the stuff is sixty to seventy years old. I'm telling you it is just vinegar. *Leave it alone.*"

She looked at Millhouse who had continued to move closer and was now standing next to her listening in on her conversation with silent interest. She continued talking into the phone. "That's not what Lord Millhouse says."

"What? You told someone else about this?"

"I needed to know the value."

"Damn it, Ann! I've told you its value. It's spoiled. *It is worthless*. Where is this Millhouse person?"

"Oh, *shit*!"

"What?"

"It's Paul! He followed us here."

"Us? Is Millhouse with you?"

Ann didn't answer, but the cell connection remained open.

Walton's motorbike sliced through the downpour and was screaming up the drive; it was a weapon aimed directly at Millhouse. Millhouse turned to run, slipping on the wet gravel as he left the cover of the *porte-cochère*, but it was useless. Seconds before running Millhouse down, Walton turned the bike and braked hard, sliding sideways in the loose gravel driveway. The bike came to a stop at the point of impact as Millhouse was knocked to the ground.

Walton was off the bike and furiously kicking Millhouse before he could recover from his fall. The rain was coming down harder. Both men were soaking wet. Millhouse, struggling to get to his feet, was unable to defend himself against the blows from Walton's boots.

Ann was screaming, "Paul, stop! Stop! It isn't what you think! The man is helping me with business! Don't hurt him anymore! Please, *stop*!"

Her message started to get through to Walton. He stopped kicking and turned toward Ann with a questioning look. At that same moment, Millhouse pulled a Kel-Tec P32 from his jacket pocket and fired.

Lord Millhouse lived by his wits. His lifestyle was not without its risks, and long ago he had learned that staying healthy meant always carrying protection. The little pistol that had saved his skin more than once weighed only 6.6 ounces—9.4 ounces fully loaded. Given its small size, the Kel-Tec P32 was easily concealed except in a Speedo.

Walton looked stunned at the sound of gunfire. The first shot was wide, the second hit home—but barely. Walton grabbed his left side where it felt as if someone had stuck him with a hot iron. The bullet did little more than graze his left side, passing through a layer of fatty tissue without hitting bone or harming muscle. It burned like hell. He slumped to his knees, not knowing if the wound was serious or not.

Ann was screaming again, but this time it was at Millhouse. "Stop! Stop for God's sake! Don't kill him!"

Lord Millhouse was quickly on his feet. He looked wild. His hair was matted and rainwater dripped from his face. His clothes were soaked; his shirt stained from his fall. The P32 was still in his hand. He used the pistol like a pointer waving it in Walton's direction as he declared, "That SOB attacked me! I should kill his ass!"

Ann took a step back, a startled expression on her face.

Millhouse realized why. With the adrenaline rush, Lord Millhouse, aka Charles Collier, had forgotten his English accent.

Clearly feeling threatened, Ann demanded, "Who are you?"

Giving up the ruse, he growled, "Someone you don't want to mess with. Get your damn boyfriend out of here before I decide to rid the earth of *both* of you."

Ann was not going to argue with a man holding a gun. Still clutching her phone, she hunched over against the rain with one arm under Walton's shoulder to support him as she led him to her car. She didn't take the time to inspect his wound but assumed she needed to get him to the hospital.

Ann drove out of the Taylor estate trying to decide which hospital was the nearest. She turned left and headed for Vanderbilt's ER.

— ʃ —

When he heard the two gunshots through the phone, Eli bolted from his office and headed for his car in the basement garage of the office building. He kept shouting into his phone, hoping to get Ann's attention. As he entered the underground garage, he lost his phone signal.

— ʃ —

For Charles Collier, aka Lord Millhouse, his Nashville stay was over. He needed to leave town and leave in a hurry. Money would be a concern. He probably shouldn't go back to his hotel. He decided to load some of the wines in the trunk of the rented Jaguar. Three or four cases should bring somewhere between a quarter and a half million dollars from the right buyers. He pulled his car under the *porte-cochère*, getting as close to the entrance of the house as he could. He worked as fast as he could. Still hurting from the fall, he could only carry four bottles at a time, which meant twelve painful trips to and from the basement cellar. The trunk was full enough, and he was exhausted. He decided not to go back for the large heavy bottle he had lugged only as far as the top step of the cellar stairs.

He took a few minutes in his car to catch his breath and finalize a plan. *I need to head south,* he thought, *to Miami. That's where I can sell this stuff for top dollar and then head to South America.* The more he thought about it, the more torn he became. The wine in the trunk of the Jag was a trifling amount compared to what was still in that cellar. He couldn't just walk away. He needed to find out if Sims or her boyfriend had gone to the police. If not, then there was time. If he had to kill Sims or that asshole who tried to run him down, it would be a pleasure.

The more he thought about it, the more convinced he was that they would not go to the police. The man would be too busy licking his wounds, and Sims would be mothering him. Collier made his decision. First, he would hide the wines he already had—a storage place somewhere out I-24 on the way to Florida. Then he would double back to Nashville for a truck and a couple of men. The rain wouldn't make it easy. Driving was terrible, and they were starting to close some roads because of high water levels. But the rain was good cover. People were trying to stay out of it. No one was going to be coming to the Taylor place in this rain. No one had a reason to, other than Sims. *If she shows up, it will be the last thing she does—bang! Sorry*

you pretty thing, but you shouldn't have gotten in my way.
Collier smiled at his little joke, started the Jag, drove off,
and turned right. He would take Hillsboro to Old Hickory
and cross over to I-24.

— ✗ —

Paul had recovered from the shock of being shot and
determined that his wound was not serious. It was bleeding, but not heavily. He used his handkerchief to apply
pressure to stop the blood loss.

"Where are we going?"

"To the hospital."

"No. Go to your place, Ann."

"You need a doctor!"

"No, I don't. This is just a flesh wound. It's not serious.
Besides, what would we tell them in the emergency room?
You really want to see your name in the paper tomorrow
linked to a shooting? Just go to your place and we'll get
this thing bandaged."

Ann wasn't sure what to do. She hadn't thought about
the police. Paul was right; the first thing the hospital would
do was report the gunshot wound to the police. But what
about Lord Millhouse—or whatever his name was? Were
they just going to let him get away with it—whatever his
game was? She realized her phone was off. It must have
gotten turned off in the melee. She turned it on, and immediately it rang.

"Where are you?" Eli sounded desperate.

"I have Paul in the car. He's been shot."

"Is it serious?"

"No, he said the bullet must have passed through the flesh—nothing really serious or dangerous."

"Where are you going?"

"I guess to my place."

"Who the hell shot him?"

"Lord Millhouse—but I don't think that's really his name."

"Ann, what in the hell is going on?"

"Eli, the rain—I have to drive now. I have to concentrate on the road."

"I'll meet you at your place."

"No. I don't want you there."

"What do you mean?"

"I have to think this through. I don't understand you anymore. You knew about the wine, didn't you?"

"Ann, we have to talk."

"Not yet, not until I can think straight."

"Ann, call me when you get home. Call me before you do anything crazy."

"You mean like tell the heirs that there is a fortune they don't even know about in that old house?"

"Ann, I told you the stuff is spoiled. Promise that you will talk to me first." The line went dead; the connection between the phones had been lost again.

The rain was coming down so hard now that Ann had trouble seeing the cars in front of her. Everyone had slowed to a snail's pace. Water was running down the streets. Oncoming traffic threw so much water on her windshield that her visibility dropped to zero as each car passed her. The drive was stop-and-go. She hoped she wouldn't get involved in a wreck and have to explain the wounded man in her car.

CHAPTER 28

Mano a Mano

The remainder of the drive was quiet except for the pouring rain and the droning of the windshield wipers. Paul was quiet, sulking—still holding his side as they arrived at the condo. Ann pressed the automatic opener and pulled into the garage. Paul needed no help getting out of the car. After Ann unlocked the door, he brushed past her and went in first. The garage entrance opened into the unit's small kitchen. He grabbed a knife from the wooden block on the counter and moved through the condo as if he lived there. He went into the bathroom and slammed the door. Walton took off his shirt. He found medical tape and gauze in the small linen closet and dressed his wound.

Ann called out from the other side of the bathroom door. "Paul, are you okay? Do you need my help?"

"I'll be out in a minute. Just leave me alone right now."

She went to the living room, sat on the sofa, and waited. Her mind was racing.

Walton came out of the bathroom without a shirt, still holding the knife. He went into Ann's bedroom and opened her walk-in closet. He selected a man's freshly laundered shirt off a hanger and put it on. He went into the living room, now holding the knife behind his back.

"Lookee here at what I found in the lady's boudoir." Sarcasm dripped from his sneer. "Nice shirt, don't you think? But it's a little big for me—"

She stood up and started to walk away from him saying, "It's Eli's."

He lunged forward and grabbed her in a one-arm chokehold around the neck. He held the knife up to her face.

"You whoring bitch. You let one of your SOB boyfriends shoot me. Now I find you're sleeping with another one! I should cut you—make you real pretty for all your men-friends."

"Paul, what are you doing? Let me go!"

He slammed her against the wall and held her there with the long blade of the kitchen knife pressed against her neck. "Or better yet, why don't I just slice your pretty little neck?"

At that moment, something powerful clamped onto the back of his neck. A strong hand gripped his forearm, pulling the knife away from Ann and back toward Paul. He dropped the knife. The arm was now around his neck jerking him backward against the man's raised knee. His back was going to break. He screamed. The man holding him threw him on the floor and kicked the knife away. Paul looked up into the murderous eyes of Eli Campbell and hoped he wasn't about to die.

"Get out of here before I tear you apart." Eli's words left no doubt in Paul's mind.

Paul got up and stumbled toward the door. He stopped and looked back at Ann. She said nothing. He opened the door and walked into the torrential rain and standing water. He left, but there was murder in his heart. The rain pounded his body. He needed to get back to his hotel, but how?

There was nothing to do but walk and hope to find somewhere he could call a taxi. He started walking through the complex, making his way to West End. Water was pouring down the driveways like a river. It wasn't easy to keep his balance.

A couple pulled up to the rear of what must have been their condo. The car doors flew opened. The man and woman were laughing and running for the rear entrance. She reached the door first and fumbled with her keys a moment, then unlocked it. The man was close behind, pushing her in as they both laughed loudly.

The keys were still in the condo door—left behind in what Walton assumed was the couple's excited dash for the bedroom. He looked around. No one was in sight. He retrieved the keys and searched for a car key. There wasn't one. He started to walk away but then decided against it. He quietly entered the condo. He could hear the couple. They had made it to the bedroom, leaving a trail of rain-soaked clothes on the floor—first shoes, then shirt, blouse, skirt, and trousers—the man's trousers. Walton picked up the pants. He patted the pockets and felt for keys. Success! He slowly backed out of the house with the trousers in his hand.

Outside, he retrieved the keys, tossed the trousers behind a bush, and waded quickly to the car, a Chevrolet

Malibu. He started the engine and headed for Opryland Hotel. The car would get lost in the hotel's enormous parking lot. Tomorrow he would find a way to the Taylor place and reclaim his motorcycle.

Right now, he had some thinking to do. No one was going to push him around like that. There were three people he owed some payback.

The going was slow on the interstate and then on Briley Parkway. Police cars were blocking some exits, apparently because of high water levels. The radio announcer was reporting on flooded streets and the evacuation of low-lying residential areas. Things were getting serious. Several times the Malibu hit high water that acted like a low wall—abruptly slowing the car's forward movement. Paul was afraid the car might stall, leaving him stranded in a stolen vehicle. He turned the radio to another station.

The mayor of Nashville was speaking: "Frankly, we have never seen a storm like this. A large portion of Davidson County has been impacted by floodwaters, and we expect it to get worse as the day continues. All our major creeks and the Cumberland River are near flood level, if not already there. The ground is entirely saturated, and the rain continues to fall. There's nowhere for the water to go. Our emergency responders have been able to handle all requests for services so far. But we need to be prepared to bring in any additional resources that are necessary to keep our citizens safe as we ride out the rest of this weather event. Our emergency responders have conducted more than 150 water rescues since the rain first started. We expect to see additional flooding as the rain continues. We urge all residents to take this situation extremely seriously and heed our warnings to stay off the roads."

Paul made it to the exit for the hotel. Traffic lights were out and only one lane was open. Police in full rain gear were directing traffic in and out of the hotel's entrance.

Next came the news anchor's voice: "The rainstorms that pushed into the area have dropped fifteen inches on Middle Tennessee, and the rain is continuing. We have received word that sections of Interstate 24 near Bell Road are under water. Rescue workers are trying to reach trapped motorists. According to Craig Owens, one of many Metro workers staffing OEM's Emergency Operations Center—which pulls together major city services like police, fire, and EMS—water is coming up through the storm drains downtown. Several downtown streets are closed because of the flooding, and the National Weather Service has posted flood warnings for the entire area, with forecasts ranging between five to eight additional inches of rain."

Paul turned off the radio. "Who gives a shit? Maybe this whole damn city will drown. It would be fucking okay with me!" The policeman waved him through the intersection and he turned into the hotel entrance.

CHAPTER 29

The Partnership

Paul had run. He was a coward. Ann had learned that about him years ago. Even when he had the knife at her throat, she knew he didn't have the backbone or guts to go through with his threats. He was all bluff.

But the man standing in front of her now was not a coward. There was no bluff in Eli and now *he* had the knife. His face was hard. His breathing was fast and short as if he had been running. His clothes were soaked from the rain. He made no effort to wipe away the beads of rainwater running down his face. He stood like someone ready for a fight—legs spread apart, hands at his side, the knife held tightly in his hand with its point to the floor.

He said nothing, and Ann realized that what she said and did next would forever change things. He could kill her. And she believed he would. But there was another way. One she had been running from. One she knew deep inside that, in the end, she wouldn't be able to avoid. This thing was always going to overtake her. She had known it.

"Okay, Eli, I give up. I don't know why I've been so stupid. We have two fortunes at our fingertips. I must have been crazy to think I could give either away and simply be a lady lawyer. Why would anybody want to do that? I was just being a naïve, stupid little girl, wasn't I?" She reached out with both hands, placing them on his cheeks. Her thumbs were under his eyes and gently wiped the rain off his face. His face softened. He turned and placed the knife on the table behind him. Then he turned back to face her, pulled her to him, and they kissed.

There was no turning back now. She had hoped it could be different. But hope was all it could be. There was no running away from her past—no righting the wrongs. Not anymore. She would continue living her lie, but now she would be party to even worse things. And, it wasn't over. She knew there would be many more bad things. She and Eli were now partners.

CHAPTER 30

No Divorce

The Opryland Hotel has almost three thousand rooms and has to accommodate even more cars because it is a convention center. Its parking areas are more like a sports stadium's—all outdoor parking, no parking garages.

Paul's plan had been to park the Malibu as far from the hotel entrance as he could. Because of the heavy rain, that plan had to change slightly. He just took the first space he saw. It wasn't close to the hotel so he had a considerable amount of ground to cover on foot and nothing to protect him from the torrential downpour. Not that it mattered—he was already soaked.

After parking the car, he tried to remember what he had touched. The rain would have washed away any prints on the outside, but what about the inside of the car? He looked around for something to use to wipe off the steering wheel. In the backseat, he found a baseball cap with the Nashville Sounds logo. He used it to wipe down the car. Then he put on the cap, took the keys, and jumped into the rain.

He knew he wouldn't be the only hotel guest looking like a drowned rat. Even if he had an umbrella, the rain was too heavy for it to do any good, and the water in places was over the top of his shoes. Running didn't help because of all the splashing, so he hunched over against the rain and waded toward the hotel's Cascades entrance. As he passed a pickup truck with Michigan plates, he threw the keys to the Malibu into the cargo bed. They wouldn't be found before the owner was back in his home state. The keys splashed. The cargo bed was full of water.

As he got to the hotel entrance, the valet staff was dressed in full rain gear—hood, jacket, pants, and boots. They had positioned two large canvas laundry containers near the door—one for fresh towels and another for used ones. Arriving guests were quickly ushered out of their cars and through the door. The valets draped the car seats in towels before sitting in the cars to drive them to the parking area.

When a doorman saw Paul headed for the door, he grabbed two towels and handed them to Paul, apparently hoping he could soak up enough of the rainwater that he wouldn't leave a trail of wet shoe prints as he walked across the lobby. It was too late from the look of things. The carpet was already water-stained and muddy.

Paul wiped his face, arms, and shirt with one of the fluffy white towels. He used the other in an effort to soak up water from his trousers and shoes. He tossed the used towels and the Sounds cap into the dirty laundry container and took another from the doorman. With the dry towel draped over his shoulders, Paul walked across the lobby. He took the elevator to his room, but he wasn't ready to call it a night.

He stripped in the bathroom and took a hot shower while carefully protecting the wound on his side the best he could. Then he put on the plush white terry cloth robe with the hotel logo on it. He lay down on the bed, immediately got up, opened the minibar, and chugged a beer. Then he opened two small bottles of Jack Daniels and poured the whiskey into a glass. Paul sat on the side of the bed, sipped the liquor, and planned his next move.

The maid had turned down the bed and there was a local newspaper, a special edition, at the foot of the bed. The front page was covered with pictures and stories about the rain and predictions of a major flood event. On page two, there was a photo of a funny-looking man with a bow tie. The caption read "Tea Party Delegate Murdered at Local Hotel." He scanned the article, stopping at the name of the delegate—*Eugene Sims!*

Walton smiled. *My little lady is still worth sixty million dollars, and I'm still her husband! Well, bitch, you can definitely forget about that divorce. Little lady, from here on, it is going to be until death do us part.* He laughed, then swung his legs up onto the bed, lay back, took another sip of whiskey, and fell asleep with the lights on and the half-full glass of Jack still in his hand.

Paul woke up to a ringing phone and someone pounding on his door. Half dazed from being awakened from a sound sleep, he went for the door first. The Jack Daniels spilled onto the bed. A Gaylord bellman stood at the door. "I'm sorry, sir, but the hotel is being evacuated. We need you to go downstairs immediately. There are buses waiting to take you to shelter on higher ground."

"Higher ground?"

"Yes, sir. The levees are leaking and could fail at any minute. The danger is critical, sir."

"Clothes . . . I have to put on some clothes. Give me five minutes."

"Sir, this is a *real* emergency. Please hurry."

Paul closed the door and wasted no time. He put on jeans and a clean T-shirt, slipped into a dry pair of Western boots, grabbed his backpack, and was out the door of his room and on his way to the lobby within five minutes.

Gaylord Opryland Hotel is located along the Cumberland River. The danger wasn't simply that the levees were leaking. The levees surrounding the building were built to sustain water rising to 422 feet above sea level. That wasn't good enough. Old Hickory Lake reached an elevation of 451.4 feet. At 452 feet, water would begin to flow over the dam. The U.S. Army Corps of Engineers opened the floodgates releasing water downstream to prevent an uncontrolled breach of the dam. The river crested at 51.9 feet, about 12 feet above flood stage.

As the last evacuation bus pulled away from the hotel, water poured over the levees filling the basin in which the hotel complex sits. The Cascades Lobby, the area where Paul and several thousand guests and hotel workers were evacuated, was quickly under ten feet of water. The air filled with the thick smell of oil as diesel fuel from the hotel generators mixed with the invading water. The Malibu and thousands of other cars in the parking lots were underwater. Some were pushed into the river by the power of the raging floodwaters and joined a dangerous flotilla of debris charging down river toward New Orleans and the mouth of the Mississippi.

"Higher ground" was McGavock High School where Paul and other evacuees spent the remaining early morning hours. A breakfast buffet set up by the hotel staff was limited to doughnuts and cereal bars. Despite the spartan conditions, Paul was lucky. He had his wallet and his cell phone. Many hotel guests, disorientated by the unexpected early morning call or knock on their door, had left everything behind in their rush to escape the rising waters.

Large television screens in the gym were showing the local news as Paul ate his Nutri-Grain bar.

Rainfall in the last 24 hours alone reached 13.86 inches in downtown Nashville. Many outlying areas experienced even higher amounts. The city of Franklin reported 14.36 inches of rain. The entire downtown of Franklin is closed—cut off by high water. Floodwaters have shut down Nashville as far as 5th Avenue. Power outages, however, have virtually closed down the city's entire business district. Creeks and tributaries are continuing to rise. Residents can expect the Cumberland and Harpeth Rivers to continue to rise even after the rainfall stops later today.

Officials with the Office of Emergency Management are urging residents to stay at home until the flooding subsides. The city's first responders are overwhelmed by calls for water rescues. If your home is safe from floodwaters, officials advise you to stay home. All city and county schools are closed, government offices are closed, and most commercial businesses are closed. Even if not directly affected by floodwaters, employees and customers are generally unable to reach businesses due to closed roads and washed-out bridges. Officials are advising everyone to stay off roadways. Many are unsafe. Those that are navigable need to remain clear for emergency vehicles.

The death toll related to the flood has risen to 18. The latest victim was a motorist caught in floodwaters on I-24 near Bell Road. Heavy accumulating rainwater had stalled and trapped 70 vehicles in the Bell Road, Antioch, area where the interstate crosses Mill Creek. According to rescue workers, the man had refused to leave his vehicle during initial evacuation of stranded motorists. Before rescue workers could return to the victim's car, the river spilled over the bridge. Fast-running floodwaters captured many cars in its path. Rescue workers eventually recovered the man's car downstream. Unfortunately, efforts to revive the driver were unsuccessful. He has been identified as a British national, Deed Millhouse.

At the sound of the announcer's words, "a British National," Paul turned to look more closely at one of the large screens. The announcer was showing a picture that looked like Millhouse. Paul whispered under his breath, "Son of a bitch!" The hotel staff had printed copies of the morning online edition of *The Tennessean* and stacked them on the tables next to the TVs. It was a six-page special edition. He grabbed one. The front page was dominated by the headline, "OVERWHELMED," and the lead story, "The Rain Just Wouldn't Stop." He found the article about the floodwater on I-24 and the picture of the motorist. Just like the Eugene Sims's murder, the man's death had been relegated to page two. There was no question about it; it was Millhouse's picture. *The bastard is dead! First the uncle, now the asshole who shot me!*

Paul walked away from the crowded gym and found a private corner in the hall of the school. He dialed her phone number again. He had been trying for several hours, but all he had gotten was a fast busy signal.

CHAPTER 31

The Next Morning

Ann was taking a hot shower. It had been a long night. Eli had been a more aggressive bed partner than ever before. Now that he had gained control over her, his approach to lovemaking changed. It was all about his satisfaction, and she was merely there for his pleasure. There was a brutality about it—and no tenderness. He demanded submission—lording over her. She had no doubt he would kill her without an ounce of remorse when he decided it was time.

The shower gave her a chance to think over her options. As far as she knew, only three people knew about the wine—Eli, Deed, and herself. She mused at the thought that she could have been a good girl. *The right thing for me to do was to confess about the mix-up following the accident. And as for the wine, the right thing was to tell the heirs. Go for the money or do the right thing. I tried, but it was an argument I was doomed to lose.*

There was just too much money involved. Nobody can be that good—not even me—at least, not at this point. I already committed one unforgivable sin when I took the place of my dead friend. They were all dead; what harm would it do? Besides, they were the ones who got it mixed up—the doctors and then later the lawyers.

The only person who would have known was Uncle Eugene. Now he's dead—a sex thing, Eli said. Yeah, right . . . I'm supposed to believe that? I'm supposed to believe Burroughs's heart just stopped all by itself right after Eli had his little talk with him? I'm just supposed to believe that a street vandal keyed Randall's car right after Eli said he would "take care of the little pipsqueak"? Eli also told me I didn't need to worry about Uncle Eugene. I don't want him to tell me . . . I don't want him to say the <u>words</u> . . . but I know, don't I? I know too much already.

So thanks to Eli, or to Eugene's would-be "man-whore," I am still worth sixty million dollars—or will be in a couple of months. That should be good enough for the bank when I approach them for a loan to bid on the Taylor property. Of course, I will have to use a broker, a surrogate, to do the bidding. As Eli knew, it would not do for the attorney who handled the process to also purchase the property. Well, the worm has turned. If I can get the wine, just maybe I will have a chance to get away from Eli, from Paul—from everyone and everything.

Poor Eugene. I could have made him an offer, one just between us. He could have avoided any taxes. If he went along with it, we would both be rich. He wouldn't have turned down the offer. I'm sure of it. If he didn't agree, I wouldn't admit to a mix-up—I would fight him if he tried *to prove otherwise. It would take years of court battles, and much of the estate would be eaten away in legal costs. No, Eugene would have gone along with it. Eli made that unnecessary, but he also took away my option to clear things up and clean the slate. Now there may be no way out for me.*

Sixty million dollars is a lot of money. I could even walk away from the wine thing and be happy with my sixty million except for two people—Eli and Paul. But I can handle Paul. He thinks small. A few million every now and then would buy his silence. I would be his goose that lays golden eggs, and he would not want anything to happen to his goose. Eli is different. The man actually feels something for me—enough to kill for me.

But now I have made myself a complication for him—and a coconspirator, a partner. What is the saying? Oh yeah, What is mine is mine, and what is yours is mine too. That's the way it is—I'm Eli's and so is my sixty million dollars and my wine. No matter what he feels for me, he will kill me. I know he will. It is just a matter of time. Of course, he has to get rid of Millhouse and Paul first, so I have some time to think. It has to be him or me.

Ann got out of the shower and heard her cell phone ring. She had left it in the bedroom and Eli answered it.

Paul wasn't surprised. *The SOB stuck around to collect his prize—my wife—after running me out of the condo!* "So you finally decided to answer the damn phone—or I should say *my* phone!"

"What the hell are you talking about?"

"I have been trying to call Ann for hours."

"Look, stupid, the system must be overloaded. I'm surprised you got through at all, and frankly, we would just as soon you hadn't."

"Screw the damn phone. Come to think of it, I guess that is what you have been doing to my lovely wife?"

"You mean your about-to-be ex-wife, don't you?"

"No, Mr. Managing Partner. I mean the wife I will have until death do us part. May I speak to her, please?"

Ann was now standing next to Eli, a towel wrapped tightly around her. Eli handed her the phone.

"Paul, is that you?"

"Yes, my sweet. I just read about the untimely death of your favorite uncle."

Ann was silent.

"Yeah, I thought you and your friend might already know about it. Quite a coincidence, don't you think? You know this changes things."

"In what way, Paul?"

"You are worth sixty million dollars again, and I am still your husband. I will be damned if I will let you divorce me."

"How much do you want?"

"I decided I want it all. I want you, and I want us to live happily ever after off *our* sixty million."

"That isn't going to happen, Paul."

"Oh, yes it is, my lovely, or I will let the secret out of the bag. Somebody is going to hang for murder—that wouldn't happen to be you, would it, sweetie?" He waited for her to say something.

"Paul, you are crazy if you think I had anything to do with that."

"Yeah, right. It is just another one of those *isolated incidents*—a coincidence. Here is the deal. You are going to get rid of Mr. Managing Partner. If you have been listening to the news, you know Opryland Hotel flooded; what you don't know is that I'm moving in with my wife tonight."

"Paul, you can't do that—not tonight. We have to talk some more first."

"Oh, yes I can, baby. Shall I come to your office to pick up a key to the place?"

"No. Let me call you back after I have checked my schedule."

"I'll give you two hours. If I haven't heard from you by then, I will be knocking on your office door—assuming, of course, that your office isn't one of those in the middle of the Cumberland River. Oh, by the way, here is some more great news for you. That shit-ass lord of yours won't be shooting at anyone ever again."

"What do you mean?"

"Look on page two of the paper."

"Don't be stupid! I don't have a paper, and I rather doubt that the delivery man will be wading to my door."

"There's a picture of him in his Jaguar stuck in rising water on I-24. The paper says before they could get him to leave his car, the river got him—tried to send him to New Orleans. So, one loverboy is down. Now all you need to do is dump that managing partner of yours. From now on, it's going to be just the two of us, you and me—just one happily married couple."

"Oh, my God!"

"I tell you what—forget the office. As I said, it's probably in the middle of the river. Pick me up at McGavock

High School. That's where the hotel has taken us." Walton looked at his watch. "It is a little past 7:00. I'll be out front at 9:30. Don't be late, little wifey."

"Have you looked outside? Paul, the whole city is turning into a lake. How do you expect me to get to you?"

"Rent a boat if you have to, sweetheart. But unless you want to hang for that trumped-up story about how poor Eugene got rubbed out, you better find a way to pick me up. I'm not sleeping on a cot in a goddamn school gym when I've got you, sweetie baby." Paul ended the call.

Eli was standing next to her. She looked at him. The frightening image of the drowning was in her head as she put a hand up to her mouth and managed to say into it, "Millhouse is dead—a flood victim."

Eli wasn't bothered by the thought of a drowning man. He smiled at the thought of a problem solved. "Good riddance; Mother Nature has saved us the trouble."

"Eli, Paul thinks I—or we—had something to do with Eugene's death. But with Eugene out of the way, he knows I will keep the money. Now he says he will no longer agree to a divorce."

"He is a problem, Ann—just another problem we have to solve."

"I'm supposed to pick him up at 9:30. He plans to move in with me. He told me to get rid of you. He thinks he can blackmail me about Eugene."

"Maybe we can let Mother Nature do us another favor. I bet the creek that runs along the Taylor property is a raging river right now. After we pick him up, I want us to go to the Taylor place."

"What do I tell him?"

"Look, you said the guy left his motorcycle there. Tell him he has to get it and take it back to your place. You know—the auction. You can't have the bike there."

"I meant about you. He isn't expecting you to be with me when I pick him up."

"We will think of something."

"Eli, what are you planning to do when we get to the Taylor place?"

"Maybe we can scare him away."

Ann was afraid Eli was planning more than just to scare Paul. But what else could she do? She couldn't stand the thought of playing wife to Paul—not anymore. And for now, she had to let Eli set the rules. She had no other options.

Her cell phone beeped. It was another text message from Mark Rollins. She had ignored the others and decided to do the same with this one. She didn't want to talk to Mark. They weren't on the same side anymore. She needed to figure out a way to get them to leave her alone—all of them, Rollins and that Sparrow woman. Things had changed. She had crossed a line, and there was no way back.

Ann got dressed. She and Eli left to pick up Paul.

Chapter 32

Assembling the Case Team

I was in the air on my way back to Nashville at 8:00 the next morning. The Challenger 300 can fly in and out of airports with runways as short as four thousand feet. The takeoff out of Reagan was short and steep over the Potomac, followed by a quick turn south and west toward Nashville.

I had been trying to find Ann Sims for hours, using everything except smoke signals, to no avail. Both landlines and cell phones were useless. All calls simply returned system busy signals. Text messages were getting through with long delays, but Sims was not responding. I had managed to reach Sarah, but we have a hardened phone thanks to the spooks at the CIA. Sarah had the same problem with busy signals when calling locally. The flood was taking out the phone system. What was left of the infrastructure couldn't handle the kind of traffic you would expect in a widespread disaster, and that's what the Nashville area was experiencing.

Sarah told me that our son, Daniel, and his family had moved in with us. Apparently, they just narrowly made it out of their neighborhood before flooding cut all access to their house. The road always floods between their home and Old Hillsboro Road, cutting off that route. The bridges over the Harpeth at Sneed Road and Moran Road were both out. While their house was perfectly safe, Daniel and his family would have had no way in or out.

I also managed to reach Sims's secretary, Judy Graves, by text message. The last time she had talked to her boss was yesterday. Sims had been on her way to the Taylor estate. Since then, Judy had not been able to contact Ms. Sims. Judy knew the Taylor place—a relative had worked on the estate years ago. According to Judy, a creek that feeds into the Harpeth River runs along one side of the place. As far as she knew, it had never flooded, but we had never seen rain like this. She clearly was concerned about her boss. The Harpeth had overrun its banks all along the river, and it was *still* raining. Her concerns heightened mine. Judy's last text message to me read: "The flood is enough to worry about, but I don't feel comfortable with her at that old house. For more reasons than just the flood, it isn't safe." It was a curious message. What were the "more reasons"?

It was time to assemble the case team. Even if we can't do it face-to-face, we have the technology to work together anywhere—and this was the time to use it. Nikto communicators issued by Bryan to everyone on the case team are similar to the Nextel phones used by police, except for two important differences. Nextel systems are limited to a particular geographic jurisdiction and use traditional cell technology combined with radio relay stations. The Nikto doesn't depend on unreliable earthbound systems. It is a satellite system. A Nikto group can connect with each other no matter where they are on the planet. I slipped the earpiece of the Nikto system over my ear and said, "Call the team."

The first person to speak was Bryan, "Yo, Chief, what's up?"

"I am. About forty thousand feet up and on my way home. Tony, Mariko, are you both online?"

Tony said, "I'm here, Mr. R."

Mariko answered, "Standing by, Boss."

The next to speak was Sam Littleton, "Mark, I have been trying to reach you. My bad for not using this Nikto thing."

"Why, Sam? Do you have something new?"

"I think you have trouble in Music City, my friend. Am I right in assuming that a Eugene Sims would have some connection with your Ms. Sims?"

"He's her estranged uncle. They haven't seen each other in fifteen or more years."

"Well, they are not going to break that record. They won't be seeing each other again—not in this lifetime."

"You mean he is dead?"

"Looks like murder."

"When and where?"

"Maids found him in his hotel room yesterday morning before all the flood confusion. Of course, with all the rain and concern about the river, there was nothing in the news until now."

"The Opryland Hotel?"

"Right . . . Mark, how did you know?"

"I had a drink with him at the hotel yesterday. But, Sam, we believe Ann Sims's husband, Paul Walton, had checked into Opryland."

"That's quite a coincidence!"

"You and I both know there is no such thing as a coincidence when dealing with murder. But just the same, we are only speculating about Walton. We think he checked in using the alias William Darcy."

"Mr. Darcy—Elizabeth Bennett's aloof gentleman friend? Okay . . . but, Mark, what is the connection to the husband?"

"Sam, he's a professor specializing in British literary masterpieces."

"Okay—seems a little far-fetched to me, but I'll buy it for now. You think this Paul Walton would have some reason to do in his wife's uncle?"

"I don't know, Sam, but according to Ann Sims, Walton is a dangerous man. He is the threat that we have been protecting her from."

"Well, assuming that Walton is involved—or even if he isn't—and the murder is somehow connected to your lady, you better find her quick and put her under wraps until the police catch the murderer."

"You are right about that. I've been trying all morning but can't reach her. That is why I activated the case room team."

Bryan spoke up, "Chief, I can relieve your concern about the woman's safety on two counts."

"Give it to me."

"First, you were right about your British lord. He wasn't who he pretended to be. Lord Millhouse is one *Charles Russell Collier* who grew up in Boston. Had a rap sheet a yard long as a scam artist. No big dollars—he just cheated old people out of a few hundred at a time. Then in 2000 at twenty, he married a forty-year-old widow and cleaned out her bank accounts, jewelry, furs, etc. She went to the police, and Collier disappeared. Warrants are still outstanding for grand larceny. Apparently, he fled to England and played the role of a rich American trust-fund type. The guy was handsome, so he didn't have any problems separating older English widows from their inheritance. I guess the guy picked up his English accent while living there. Things must have gotten hot for him over there because he came back to the States and assumed the persona of a British lord.

"However, while all that is interesting, the gentleman—if you want to call him a gentleman—is no longer with us. He was a flood victim. I can give you the details if you want them, but suffice it to say, the floodwaters got him on I-24 near Bell Road. It looks like he was leaving town."

Rollins let that sink in before he said, "That is a horrible thing to happen to anyone, even someone like him. But, you are right; it is one less person we have to be concerned about. What about our angry policeman?"

"That's the other one we can take off the list, at least for right now. We were tracking new phone number assignments by the major cell phone companies and had a hit on Verizon. Purdue purchased a smartphone. Before the cell system went nuts on us, we were able to lock onto it by satellite. We are monitoring his movements in real time, and I can activate his phone without his knowledge anytime I want to. That means I can hear everything going on around him—hear any conversations he is having or those of any people close by. Right now, he is being a good citizen. He is in Bellevue, in the Temple Road area, helping first responders. That area is one of the hardest hit by the flood. You have some houses that are completely underwater—a lot of people stranded. Rescuers are trying to get to all of them in time. So, he's a busy boy."

"Good for him. But, Bryan, we can't forget about him. Stay alert just in case anything changes. That just leaves us with a missing lady who we are supposed to be protecting, and a missing abusive husband that we are supposed to be protecting her from. Someone, who I might add, may have murdered Eugene Sims. Damn it, Bryan, I feel like a blind man—what has happened to our intelligence assets?"

"Chief, Big John just texted me. He has been on the phone with our guys at CSI, and he has an update on the Eugene Sims murder. He was drugged with Rohypnol."

"He overdosed?"

"That's not my understanding. Let me bring John online."

Littleton interrupted, "Wait, Bryan, remind me who John is, and what's his connection with CSI."

"He's John Felts. We call him 'Big John.' You met him when we were working on the Puppeteer case."

"Oh yes, now I remember—no wonder you call him Big John. If anyone deserves the 'big' moniker, it's him!

As I remember it, he worked over at Metro's CSI unit, all four hundred pounds of him, before joining your team."

"That's right. Let me put him online . . . Okay, John, you are connected to the case room team. What are they telling you over at CSI?"

After a second, John said, "Good morning, everyone. I think the killer wants us to think Mr. Sims overdosed on the date rape drug, but that's not the way CSI sees it. According to my contact, he appears to have been asphyxiated after the Rohypnol knocked him out. The police arrested a known male prostitute who works local hotels. He goes by the name Billy Lovejoy. They had him on security cameras leaving one of the bars in the Opryland Hotel with the murder victim. Problem is the murder doesn't fit the guy's modus operandi. This Lovejoy swears his target was alive when he left him, and frankly, my contact says the detectives on the case tend to believe him. Right now, they don't have any other suspects so they are still holding Lovejoy, and the district attorney plans to charge him with manslaughter. The cleaning service found the victim's wallet in a trash receptacle next to the elevator right where Lovejoy said he tossed it. Cash was gone, but Lovejoy apparently doesn't deal in credit cards or IDs. They were all there as well as a photo of the victim and a young girl. The back of the photo identifies her as Ann Sims and the date on the back is September 19, 1999, along with the words '14th birthday.' "

"John, this is Mark. Good job as usual."

Mariko interjected, "Will someone make me understand why Eugene Sims's death is a concern for us? Why would her husband want to kill her uncle?"

Sam Littleton said, "I'm with you, Mariko. What is this guy? Is Walton a crazed killer or something?"

Rollins answered, "Sam, I'm not totally convinced yet that Walton is the killer. I do know that he's the jealous type. He hasn't taken the separation from his wife well—appears to be stalking her. The divorce is becoming final in a few days. And we know that in an abusive situation, that is the most dangerous time for the wife—in this case, Ann Sims. But killing the uncle doesn't fit. At the same time, Walton appears to have checked into the Opryland Hotel under an assumed name, and shortly thereafter, the uncle shows up dead. We have to assume there's a connection."

Tony said, "Well, Mr. R, you know what they say about assuming: It can make an *ass* out of yo*u* and *me.*'"

I let Tony's remark slide. "Bryan, let's go back to the photo in the uncle's billfold. If I recall, Sims's fourteenth birthday would have been only a couple of years before the big wreck when her parents were killed."

"Right, Chief. Three were killed—her parents along with another girl traveling with them, a friend of Ann's. Cassie Poole was her name. According to the reports we found, there was heavy fog on the interstate just outside Monteagle on the downside of the mountain. Several cars were involved along with a propane tanker. There was an explosion. There was nothing left of the car or its passengers, except for Sims. She was the sole survivor. She was the only one not wearing her seat belt and was thrown out of the vehicle.

"Luck or faith was on her side that day. She was in bad shape, however. The people at Emerald Hospital in Sewanee kind of adopted her. According to the news reports, the girl was in a coma for two weeks. By the time she was back in the world of the living, her parents and her best friend were already laid to rest. The county took care of the remains—there wasn't enough to bury. The *Sewanee Mountain Messenger* had an ongoing column that reported on the young girl's progress. She was 'the girl without anyone.' That was the storyline. No one came to visit Ann Sims except lawyers representing the family's estate."

"Mr. R, if I remember our conversation correctly, that's why Eugene Sims thought Ann didn't want to see him—because he never visited her in the hospital."

"That's right, Tony. That's what the uncle told me when I visited with him. But you know, maybe there was another reason—" Rollins took a second to align his thoughts. "I know it is a bit crazy, but what if Ann didn't survive the car wreck? You read about things like that—where identities get mixed up. Maybe Ann Sims is not who we think she is. Maybe she is the other girl—Cassie Poole. Maybe that's why she was always avoiding her uncle. And, now that uncle was finally going to meet with her—face-to-face. If she isn't really Ann Sims, that big estate she was about to inherit would be out the door. That would certainly give us a motive for murder. Sam, you guys are experts at this. Can you age the photo and compare it to a picture of the person we have been calling Ann Sims?"

"Sure, that won't be a problem. However, first you have to get the picture to me, and it's in Metro's hands from what Big John said."

Big John replied, "Don't worry about that. It won't be a problem. I'll have a digital copy on its way to you within ten minutes."

Tony cut in, "Okay, so maybe we have a motive for murder, but who would the 'motivee' be?"

"Good question, Tony. Ann would have to be a candidate. Walton would also be on the list, except for the pending divorce."

"Mr. R, what if there is no divorce? Could Sims and Walton be in it together? You know, the divorce might be a ruse to throw us off the scent. Sixty million is a lot of dollars."

"I guess it is possible, Tony. But even more relevant is the question of what would happen to that sixty million dollars if something happened to Sims before the divorce. Everything would go to Walton unless there was a will to the contrary."

Bryan said, "We haven't found anything like a will in Sims's hard drives, nor has a will popped up in the places one would expect if prepared by an estate lawyer, like in the hands of an institution named as executor. But, as you know, in Tennessee you can have a handwritten will that is legal."

Mariko said, "Well, I guess we need to get off our duffs and go find your Ann Sims or Paul Walton, and we better do it pretty quick."

"Bryan, you have got to find Sims for me!"

"I'm sorry, Chief, but all our assets are off-line. We got our lock on Purdue before the flood took out most of the cell system. Now we're having trouble just making a regular call. Most of TDOT's cameras on roads and interstates are off-line. The disaster preparedness facility itself is actually underwater. Our first responders are busy rescuing people caught by rising waters. About the only way you can move around is in a boat. You've probably heard they're calling this a monumental event."

"Sounds like it's getting worse instead of better. Sam, do you have anything you can deploy to help us out?"

"Mark, to be honest, I shouldn't even be in this meeting. As you can imagine, everything we have, men *and* resources, is supporting the locals dealing with this disaster. We will work on the photograph, but other than that, this is one time you need to count us out. In fact, until things change, you need to take me out of the case room loop."

"I understand, Sam. Thanks for what you have been able to do."

"Bryan, difficulties or not, it's up to *you* to find her. What about our drones?"

"Our miniatures can't penetrate the cloud cover and rain. We have the new Hummingbird from the military. We are doing encryption tests for them, but they are ground tests only. If we fired that thing up in a civilian area, we would probably be shot by a firing squad. Besides, our Hummingbird is equipped only for clear sky operation over desert terrain. We don't have the jungle package that we would need to see through this mess."

"Bryan, the rain has to stop sometime. Also, don't our homebrew miniature predators have infrared?"

"Yes, but what good would that do us?"

"Well, at least we could monitor Sims's condo and the Taylor place so we don't have to waste boots on the ground in those areas. If we don't have images, we would at least know where they *aren't.*"

"Okay, Chief, I'll put two of them in the air over those places, ASAP. My guess is they won't last long in this weather. The rain will beat them up pretty badly."

"Keep the cameras going as well as the temperature-differential mode. If you get a body-heat image, you can take the bird down below the clouds. If we lose it, we aren't talking about a big financial loss, thanks to you and your team—so let's play it the way special ops would. You know—'one is none; two is one.' Double up. Put two birds on each location."

"Will do, Chief."

"Tony, where are you?"

"Waiting for you. The folks at Signature let me know when you lifted your wheels at Reagan, so I'm standing by."

"You're a good man. But I have another job for you. I want you to find Paul Walton. Go to the Opryland Hotel; find out what room William Darcy is in. If it really is Paul Walton, I don't want you to let him out of your sight."

"Hold it, Mr. R. Opryland is underwater. They evacuated the entire population, guests and staff, early this morning."

"The order still stands—find Paul Walton! Find out where the guests were taken. Find this Darcy person. And, Tony, if it *is* Walton, he may be dangerous."

"Mr. R, roads are closed all over the place. If they *are* in the Opryland area, getting through using the Lexus isn't going to be easy."

"Leave the Lexus for me. Check with Bobby Townsend. He runs the food service at Signature, and I happen to know he's a Harley man. Tell him who you are. Give him the matter-of-life-or-death speech and five hundred dollars to rent his bike for a few hours."

"Roger, Mr. R. If Townsend gives me any problems, I'll hotwire his Harley and let you patch things up the old-fashioned American way—more money."

"Sounds like a plan. Make it happen. And, Tony, keep in mind that it may really be a matter of life or death."

"Mariko, I need you on the 'find-Ann-Sims' team. Can you use one of your bikes?"

"Boss, I'm already mounted on my old Black Max, and I'm one wet duck. Where do you want me to start?"

"Go to her condo first. She won't be there, but maybe you will find something. Let me know if you do. Then check out the Taylor estate. Contact the law firm, if you can, to make sure she isn't at one of their locations—but the law firm is last on our list. If she's there, we can assume she's safe."

"Boss, what about a vehicle? What does she drive?"

"A red Mercedes CLK550."

Tony was still listening and said, "Well, Mr. R, one thing I can say is that is *not* the best car to be driving through high water. It's built too close to the ground."

"Nevertheless, everyone keep an eye out for it. One more thing, Mariko, as I told Tony, this may or may not be dangerous. Do you have protection?"

"Always. I may be wearing wet leather, but my Springfield EMP is resting in the inside pocket, nice and dry."

"Good. We have started our descent, and it is kind of bumpy up here, turbulence, so I'm ending this conference. Use your Nikto communicators to stay in touch with Bryan as control."

With the meeting over, I had a few minutes to think. It was curious that no one could reach Ann Sims; and, more importantly, that she had not reached out to me. She was either in trouble or maybe she was part of the trouble.

This had all started with her dog—but it quickly changed. For a moment I had thought maybe the dog had just been an excuse to get me involved. Had she manipulated me? Was I wrong about her? Maybe she is innocent. But I can't forget that sixty million dollars is a lot of money. And what is it about the Taylor estate? I don't know. I need more answers, not more questions.

I heard the wheels descend from the plane's belly, looked out the window, and said the only thing I could think of—"Holy crap!" Nashville had become an island. The city was surrounded by water. Downtown was being reclaimed by the Cumberland River.

CHAPTER 33

Sweaty Palms

It was still raining hard as the car pulled under the protective cover of the bus entrance to McGavock High School. Paul was there, waiting impatiently.

As Ann got out of the car and approached him, he began to rant, "It's about time you got here. Wait a minute! Who's that in the car? Oh, shit! What the hell is he doing here?"

"Paul, just think for a minute, will you? I could not have gotten here without his help. There's water everywhere, not to mention that trees and power lines are down. I had to have help. I'll drop him off at his car once I get back to the condo. Come on—be nice."

"We're not going to be getting along, Ann. If he puts a hand on me again, so help me, I will kill him."

"Paul, don't start something you might not be able to finish. I'm not exactly sure what Eli did in the military, but I don't think you want to find out. You've seen how quick he can be. So just be nice. Remember, I couldn't have gotten here without him, and we still need him to find our way back. If you're smart, you'll smile and thank him. Then I'll drop him off at his car, and it will be just the two of us. We can figure out where we go from there."

"There isn't any figuring to do. I told you how it is going to be."

"Paul, just get in the goddamn car."

"Open the trunk for my backpack."

"Is that all the luggage you have?"

"It is a little hard to bring a lot of things on a bike."

"Okay, Paul, I wasn't trying to be a smart-ass. The trunk space in my car is almost nonexistent. I hadn't thought about luggage until now. The backpack will fit fine but not much more. Did you have to leave anything behind at the hotel?"

"No. This is it except for a few things in the bags on my bike. I hope it's still there—at that old house."

"I'm sure it is. We're going there first so you can get it."

"What do you mean, 'we'?"

"It makes sense to go directly to the Taylor place. You can ride your bike to my condo while I take Eli to his car."

"Okay, okay, whatever—let's get it over with. The sooner I get my bike, and you get rid of the caveman, the better."

Ann opened the trunk, and Paul threw in his bag. Eli opened the passenger door and said to Paul, "You can ride shotgun. I'll squeeze into the back." He pulled the back of the passenger seat forward and climbed into the small backseat of the Mercedes.

Paul hesitated as he tried to think of a smart comeback, but surprised himself and simply said, "Thank you."

He got into the car, as did Ann. Placing her hands on the steering wheel, Ann realized her palms were sweating. As a lawyer, she had learned to control visual signs of her emotions. Look nervous in front of a jury, and you have lost. She hadn't looked or acted nervous in front of Paul, but her damp palms told the true story. She had been—and still was—extremely nervous.

Ann was sure Eli had killed before. And even though it remained unspoken, she knew Eli expected her to take part in Paul's murder. What alternative did she have? There was one—she knew there was one. It was the only way out for her. But how? How and when could she make it happen? She felt the weight of the LadySmith revolver in the purse on her lap. She had the means. What she needed was the opportunity.

— ⨍ —

Eli slapped the back of Ann's seat. "This was a bad move. We should have never gotten on 440. Interstate 24 has been shut down for two days. You would think the cops could have figured out how to reroute traffic by now. Instead, they've turned 440 into a parking lot."

Ann's irritation showed as she said, "There's been an accident, Eli! It looks like they'll have it cleared in a few more minutes."

"Yeah, there's a wreck. The idiot was trying to back up the entrance to I-24 because he didn't pay attention to the damn signs. The other fool wouldn't give in to let him back on 440—bam, bam, bam, and we have a three-car pileup. Real smart people." Eli looked around to see if there were any nosey drivers close to their car. There weren't. Most people were watching the police and the tow trucks as they worked to clear the wreck ahead of them. The rain also reduced visibility. Eli leaned forward and said, "Paul, turn on the radio. Maybe we can get a report on the roads. If we get out of this mess, I don't want to get into another one."

Paul shifted his body and reached for the radio's control panel, but his hand never made it to the power button. Eli's trained hands gripped just the right spot at the base of Paul's neck. Paul remained upright and aware for a short time but paralyzed, unable to speak or move. His vision blurred and then faded into a void of blackness. In a few more seconds, lack of blood flow shut down his brain, and his body went limp as he fell into deep unconsciousness.

As Paul slumped against the passenger door, Eli said, "I hate this damn car. When we get passed this shit, find a place to get off the interstate. Then pull over and stop so I can dump your ex-loverboy in the back, and I can move up front. I'm dying back here."

"How long will Paul be out, Eli?"

"He'll be out long enough for me to give him a shot of something that will keep him sleeping for a couple of hours. Surely we can get to the Taylor place before then."

CHAPTER 34

Back in Nashville

Tony had left Black Beauty in plain sight parked near the passenger lounge. I headed for the WH Club and called Bryan as I entered the ramp to Interstate 40.

"Chief, Judy Graves is here. I have her in the small conference room next to your office."

"Ann's secretary? What does she want?"

"She wants to see you. The woman was so distressed that she opened up to me. You're going to find her story interesting. She says Sims is in danger but that the person we should be concerned about is—get this—the firm's managing partner, Eli Campbell."

"Before we go any further with this, do we know where Eli Campbell is right at this moment?"

"No. He's another loose piece on the game board. And that's apparently what made Graves decide to come forward. No one seems to know where either Campbell or

Sims is. Everyone else at the law firm is accounted for. They've not responded to the firm's disaster protocol."

"Tell me more."

"Sims's law office is in the center of the city, which is now smack dab in the middle of the Cumberland River. They're smart people so they have plans in place for dealing with a situation like this—a control point, backup site, secure and mirrored off-site servers, call trees, emergency text, and call-out notification system, etc. By now, they expected everyone to have shown up physically at the firm's backup site or, at a minimum, established some form of communication with the firm. Everyone has followed protocol with the exception of our two missing people—Sims and Campbell."

"First things first, Bryan. I assume you're making an effort to find Campbell."

"We're working on the cell phone aspect. Service is very spotty, but we hope to get a ping that we can vector on. So far, we have nothing. All I can tell you is that we will keep trying."

"Okay. Let's get back to the secretary's story. My understanding is that Campbell and Sims had a thing going. He is not someone she was afraid of. She thought he got a little too possessive at times, but that's all. What makes Graves think otherwise?"

"I wish you were here to talk to her yourself. You'd see how uncomfortable she is talking about this. I'm not sure I have the days straight. Either yesterday or the day before, Campbell rushed out of the office in a rage about something Sims had done. Sims was at the Taylor estate and Graves thinks he left the office to confront her. Graves thinks it's something about the Taylor estate. Neither Campbell nor Sims has been seen or heard from since."

"Bryan, people get mad without killing each other. Campbell was her boss and he and Sims had been, and maybe still are, lovers. There has to be more to this than just that."

"There is, and I think that's the part that has Graves so uncomfortable. She believes Campbell may have killed one of the firm's partners."

"Shit. Why does the plot always have to get messier? Bryan I'm pulling into the back lot. Meet me in the conference room. I think I'll let Ms. Graves tell me the rest of the story herself."

"Will do, Chief. Welcome back, by the way."

CHAPTER 35

Judy's Story

"Ms. Graves, Bryan says you believe Mr. Campbell may have killed one of the firm's partners?"

"Yes."

"Tell me about it."

"I'm sorry, Mr. Rollins, this is very hard for me. Mr. Campbell has always been nice to me. And I'm Ms. Sims's legal secretary. I can't be sure I'm doing the right thing, but I just can't get this out of my mind. If I don't do anything and something bad happens, I'll never be able to live with myself. No matter what else happens, coming to you will probably cost me my job."

"May I call you Judy?"

"Of course."

"Tell me. I promise you that whatever you have to say will just be between us . . . unless it turns out that your intuition is right."

"Thank you . . . My great-grandmother worked for the Taylors. The story is that Mr. Taylor forced himself on her when she was only sixteen and got her pregnant. He was cruel to her. And if you can believe old family stories, she poisoned him with this." She held up a small purple bottle. "Please take it. I don't want it anymore."

Taking the bottle, and looking at it skeptically, Rollins asked, "This little purple bottle was your great-grandmother's?"

"Yes."

"What's in it?"

"I don't know, Mr. Rollins. Witches' brew for all I know. The story is that she made it from the leaves of the hedges that grow along the front of the Taylor place along Hillsboro Road."

"What does this have to do with Campbell?"

"I'm sorry . . . I'm rambling . . . I know. Before I was Ms. Sims's secretary, I worked for a really horrible person—Henry L. Burroughs III, a partner in the law firm. Everyone hated the man, but I was his personal slave. The day he died, he had been particularly vile, and even targeted Ms. Sims. Mr. Campbell witnessed his verbal attack on Ms. Sims. Mr. Burroughs sent me to fetch his coffee, and I had that little purple bottle. I knew how my great-grandmother must have felt. I wanted to kill him."

"Did you?"

"No, I put the bottle away. But I'm sorry to say that I spit in his coffee, and then I spit in it again. I wanted to take it to him and watch him as he sipped his precious cup of 'seasoned' coffee. But Mr. Campbell took the coffee instead."

"You mean Campbell drank it?"

"No, no, he delivered it. He told me he was going to have a talk with Mr. Burroughs and that I didn't need to worry about him anymore."

"And that's when you think Campbell killed him?"

"Yes, he was the last person to see Mr. Burroughs alive. When I went into the office later to check on him, Mr. Burroughs was dead."

"You know, Mr. Rollins, I was so ashamed that I took the empty coffee cup and saucer and hid them in my desk. I was afraid someone would want to test it and they would find my spit. That was stupid, of course. But I don't need people thinking I go around spitting in people's food."

"Don't you think Burroughs could have died naturally? People die from massive heart attacks—couldn't that have been the case?"

"Of course, it *could* be. But Mr. Campbell was in the military. He's really strong, Mr. Rollins. Just the way he said that I would never need to worry about Burroughs again frightens me when I remember it. If there were ever someone who could kill, it would be Eli Campbell. All I know is that he went into that office and the next time I entered the office, Mr. Burroughs was dead."

"Okay, let's assume for a minute that you are right about Burroughs. I still have to ask why you think he might harm Ms. Sims. I understood that they were lovers."

"You didn't see Mr. Campbell's face or the rage in his eyes when he stormed out of the office after her. I did. I was scared to death."

I got up to leave but Ms. Graves stopped me. "Please, don't go yet. I need to tell you about the Taylor place. There's something bad about it, and it has infected Ms.

Sims and probably Mr. Campbell. Whatever he was mad about, I'm sure it involved that house and the auction."

"One thing I can tell you, Judy, is that there will not be an auction—at least, not anytime soon."

"What do you mean?"

"Judy, just think. Even after the rain stops, it will be days—probably weeks or months—before Nashville gets back to normal. You can forget about the auction. It's not going to happen in the near future."

"Mr. Rollins, have you thought about that house sitting empty for more than fifty years? The carriage house is full of cars. They were new *fifty* years ago. And there's something else about the house. I don't know exactly what it is, but there's something there that Mr. Campbell wants. Something I think Ms. Sims may have discovered and, whatever it is, that's what Mr. Campbell was on a tear about."

"Well, whatever it is, it will still be there tomorrow and the next day."

"You say that, Mr. Rollins, but what happens if the creek overflows its banks?"

After our conversation ended, I left Judy with Bryan and asked him to make sure she got home or back to the law firm's backup site.

I wasn't sure how much weight to give the secretary's story, but we clearly had another loose piece on the playing board. I went into my office, shut my eyes, and tried to fit the pieces together. I had a collection of round holes and square pegs. The Taylor property was prime real estate. If the economy ever recovered, the property would become a gated community. But if she was right, there was more to the value of the Taylor place than the land and that old house. It had secrets—fifty-year-old secrets. But were they valuable secrets—a stash of silver or gold coins, old bonds or stock certificates, paintings by old masters, or simply of value only to the old man who died there? One thing I was sure of, there was not going to be an auction anytime soon. But that didn't mean the heirs wouldn't be even more anxious to cash in. I tried to call Curtis, my lawyer, and was surprised when the call actually went through.

"Curtis, I want you to buy a piece of property for me."

CHAPTER 36

Tony's Report

"Chief, it's Bryan. I'm back in the control seat. Ms. Graves was safely delivered to the law firm's backup location on the other side of Brentwood from us—one of those office buildings on Summit Place."

"Thanks, Bryan. What about Tony?"

"I'm online, Mr. R. Bryan's team did a great job guiding me around problem areas. I would still be trying to find navigable streets without their help. McGavock High School doesn't look very safe to me. It's located right in a bend of the Cumberland River, so it has water on three sides. It wouldn't take much for those Opryland evacuees to become completely cut off."

"What about Walton?"

"The hotel people have been trying to account for everyone, so it was easy to confirm that a Mr. Darcy was one of the guests who boarded the bus and was taken straight to the school from the hotel. I flashed some pictures of

Paul Walton. They identified him as their Mr. Darcy, but he's not here anymore—signed out early this morning. I asked a lot of questions and showed a lot of people his picture. I got different answers, but the majority indicated that he left early this morning in a red sports car. Someone must have picked him up because everything in the hotel parking lot is now under a lot of water."

"Tony, I think you are right. We're pretty sure his transportation is a motorcycle. He doesn't have a car, but Sims does, and it's a red sporty Mercedes. We have to assume that it was Ann, or at least her car. That makes things even more intriguing. If she was driving, why doesn't she answer my calls and text messages or those from her office? She's either deliberately avoiding any attempts to contact her, or someone—I assume Paul Walton—is not letting her communicate with us. Bryan, are you listening? We need answers! The question remains where is Ann? Where is that car? Where is Paul Walton? And now, where is Eli Campbell?"

"Chief, all I can tell you is that we are doing our best. Some assets are coming back online—a few TDOT cameras. The cell system is coming back little by little. We still don't have enough infrastructure back online to lock onto a cell phone unless we just get lucky, and then I doubt that we could hold the lock unless we have enough time to reroute to a satellite."

"Keep trying for her cell and for Campbell."

"We will, but don't forget that they may have pulled their batteries. We know Walton is a battery puller. She may have learned that trick from him."

"Mr. R?"

"Yes, Tony?"

"Whoever was driving the pick-up car has to know Nashville *very* well. With all the street closures, you don't just get in your car and drive out here. You have to hunt and pick your way through a lot of backstreets. And that Mercedes rides pretty close to the ground. If they try to cross high water, that car will become a boat and then a rock."

"Tony, I'm sure Sims knows the city pretty well, but she doesn't strike me as the kind of person who would take chances driving in this stuff, but one of our other missing persons wouldn't have any problems taking risks—Mr. Eli Campbell. Didn't any of the people you questioned give you a description of the driver?"

"No—nothing, Mr. R. No one saw or remembers seeing anyone, male or female. For all I know, there could have been several other people in the car he left in."

"Tony, what about personal effects? Did Walton leave anything useful behind?"

"No such luck. He took it all with him. Evacuees were allowed to bring one personal item and one small suitcase or bag, the size that you can carry onboard airplanes. Everything else had to be checked or left in their rooms. Darcy claimed his stuff when he signed out this morning."

"Tony, you said he signed out?"

"Right, Mr. R, I know what you're thinking. The sign-out sheet does include space for a phone or e-mail address where the individual can be contacted. Our person of interest entered an e-mail address. Care to guess?"

"Come on, Tony; just give it to me. We're running short on time."

"Darcy@pemberley.com."

"Of course it was. Our Mr. Darcy, aka Paul Walton, likes to be cute. He either is playing with us or thinks we're all just a bunch of illiterate rednecks. Pemberley House was Mr. Darcy's residence in Jane Austen's *Pride and Prejudice*."

"Mr. R, what do you want me to do now? I don't see any reason to hang around McGavock."

"Head back toward the club, but first talk to the hotel security people. Flooded or not, they probably still have some of their security staff at the hotel. If they can get to Mr. Darcy's room, have them confirm that neither his dead body nor anyone else's is inside. Let them know what we are dealing with and get an agreement from the security team that they will alert us in the unlikely event that he should return to the McGavock location—or attempt to return to the hotel property."

"You got it, Mr. R."

CHAPTER 37

CLK550

"Bryan, I don't like this. We're too good to let this happen. We need our eyes and ears."

"You're right, Chief. Let me fill you in. I sent four of our guys to the Mercedes-Benz dealer in Cool Springs to get characteristic fingerprints that identify a CLK550 configured similarly to the one owned by Ann Sims."

"How did you do that? Isn't the Cool Springs area flooded?"

"Not all of it. We did have to go through high water, and the Mercedes place isn't open for business, but we called in some chits. First, we have the advantage of having a Land Rover dealer located within walking distance of the club. They loaned us a Land Rover that can drive through almost anything. Second, the Mercedes dealer's wife is a platinum member of the WH Club. She got her husband to open up for us."

"Okay, Bryan, but how does that help?"

"Chief, we now have the unique sound pattern of its engine. We know its temperature patterns—from start-up to cooldown and with one, two, or three passengers. We also know the chemical composition of the emissions it puts into the atmosphere. We have uploaded those finger-prints to our drones. I'm keeping one each over the condo and the Taylor place, and I have the other two flying a search pattern over the extended Nashville area."

"Sounds like a pretty difficult sniffing job for our birds. You really think you can make this work?"

"As far as I know, no one has ever tried this before, but I think it could work. We're concentrating on the traffic areas where we'd expect Sims to be. That improves our odds. But we're also using facial-feature–style software to watch for CLK550s passing through any TDOT cameras that are still functioning—there are still a lot of them off-line, but we might get lucky. We also have one more trick up our sleeve. Sims's car does not have a GPS. If she did, we could track her real time. But she does have satellite radio. We hacked into her SiriusXM account. From there, we got the digital ID for the radio in her car. If they turn it on, we'll have them."

"What about Mariko? Anything from her?"

"She's at the condo on West End. Sims wasn't there, of course, but she has been giving the place the once-over. I'll get her online, and she can fill you in herself."

"Great . . . and Bryan, hang on to that Land Rover. I'm going to need it. We didn't modify Black Beauty to handle the water I've pushed her through. It was a hairy drive back to the club, and I'm afraid the going is only getting worse."

CHAPTER 38

Mariko's Report

"Boss, there were people here last night, that's clear. I would say two of them stayed all night—same bed. I'd say they slept together, but from the condition of the bed covers, the sleep part would be an overstatement. What concerns me, however, are the bloody bandages I found in the bathroom trash. There was more blood than you would expect from a little kitchen accident, so I ruled that out. I examined the discarded dressings closely and there is a small circular area darker than the rest—more blood saturation. Looks like a bullet wound to me. Just a guess, of course. I checked the bed for any signs of blood spots. I found none. If the overnighter was the wounded person, I would have expected some seepage from the dressing. So, I would speculate that there were at least *three* people here at some point last night. Two of them stayed the night—neither of them was the wounded party."

"Mariko, Sims keeps a handgun in her nightstand. Check and see if it's there."

"I don't have to look again—there is no gun there. I went through her things pretty thoroughly. I haven't run across a weapon of any kind."

"That is not good."

"There is something else, Boss. Metro was at the condo complex when I arrived. They were investigating a car theft. It seems that last night someone stole a car belonging to a unit a few doors down from Sims."

"Curious . . . I wonder if it has anything to do with the person who didn't stay the night at Sims's place—the wounded one. Find out the details, Mariko. Let me know ASAP if it comes close to being a red sports car."

Bryan interrupted, "Chief, I have Sam Littleton on the line."

"Okay, put him through."

"Mark, I have two things for you. First, there is no possible way that the fourteen-year-old girl in that photograph and your Ann Sims are the same person. They are not even close—totally different bone structure. I'll send you the aged photograph. And, our guys pulled up some photos of the other girl in the wreck from the newspaper morgue."

"Cassie Poole?"

"Yes, we aged her photo, and it is spot-on. Your Ann Sims is actually Cassie Poole."

"I was beginning to think that would be the case, Sam. If she had met with Eugene Sims as he had asked, our Ann Sims could have kissed her sixty-million-dollar inheritance good-bye."

"That's right, Mark. It sounds like a motive for murder to me."

"Yes, but we still have to find 'who done it.' "

"Mark, don't you think girls commit murder?"

"Sure they do, but more often than not, they seduce some poor slob into doing the dirty deed for them. You've seen our imposter. She could seduce a lamppost! She got me to investigate a dog murder, didn't she? She wouldn't even have to *tell* someone to do it. She could have just cried on someone's shoulder until the shoulder's owner decided to do it on his own."

"Well, I have to leave this for you to solve, Mark. I've got other priorities right now. However, I do have a couple more pieces of intel before I get off the line."

"What's that?"

"They fished your phony British lord's Jaguar out of Mill Creek and its trunk was full of wine."

"Wine? Do you know any details?"

"Mark, I understand most of the labels had washed off. Those that survived were badly damaged and falling apart. The officer on the scene reported that they were old wines—he did not specify dates or names. Is this making any sense to you?"

"It might answer a question I've been wrestling with. I'll tell you later."

"Well, here's another answer for you that's looking for the right question. Maybe you have it."

"What is that, Sam?"

"We also found a small pistol, a .32 caliber. It had been fired—two rounds."

"Would it surprise you if I said I have the right question for that answer?"

"Not at all, Mark. You can tell me about it over a cold beer sometime. Right now, I have to move on."

Sam signed off, and Mariko asked, "What do you want me to do next, Boss?"

"Head for the Taylor place. Give me a call when you get there."

"Chief?"

"Yes, Bryan?"

"We finally got a hit on the Mercedes. Our drones picked up a scent that I feel sure is the car we are looking for. It was on 440 near the exit to I-24. It appeared stationary for a few minutes, started to move, and then we lost it. While it was still stationary, we got an infrared reading, and there are definitely three people in the vehicle. I would say it is headed in our direction."

"Good! Bryan, I think the picture is getting clearer. We have had three people off the radar screen—our Ann Sims; her husband, Paul Walton; and Eli Campbell, Sims's coworker and probably her lover. It appears that all three are now in Sims's car headed in our direction—the direction of the Taylor place."

"Chief, it has to be intentional that they tried to make themselves invisible."

"Yes, Bryan, one or more of them wants it that way."

"Okay, Chief, I got it, but why is that?"

"Because one or more of them plans to do something that's bad—like murder. And I think it's happening right now, or maybe it has already happened."

"Chief, you think it's because of something hidden away in that old mansion?"

"Yes and no, Bryan. Yes, there is something inside that place that is so valuable that one person has died trying to get it, and one or more of these three people would murder for it—and probably will before this finishes playing out. But Bryan, we also still have the sixty-million-dollar inheritance at play here. Let's go over what we know:

- The man who could have exposed Ann Sims as Cassie Poole was murdered.
- Three people go off the radar screen.
- A phony British lord is pulled out of Mill Creek with a trunk load of old wine and a concealed weapon that has been fired.
- Mariko finds evidence that at least three people were at Sims's condo last night.
- She finds bandages that suggest one of the three had been shot.
- She also finds evidence that two people, other than the one wounded, spent the night at Sims's condo sharing the same bed.
- Someone steals a car from a condo practically next door to Sims's—probably our wounded person.
- Two people, Sims and Campbell we assume, pick up Sims's husband—now they are three again. The three are now headed toward the Taylor place.

"What does that tell you, Bryan?"
"That they are all in it together?"

"Wrong—there is one other thing I did not mention. Paul Walton is also a threat to Sims's inheritance. He probably knows Ann's secret. But even if he doesn't, by fighting the divorce he could upset everything."

"Okay, Sherlock, who is the bad guy?"

"They are all bad, Bryan. But right now, I would say the person in the most danger is Paul Walton. We know Paul wasn't the one sleeping with Ann last night and that means Eli was. If Paul didn't kill Eugene Sims—and I no longer think he did—then I would say that, as Sims's unwanted husband, he is next on the list of those who must go. If he isn't already dead, he will be soon if we don't stop it."

"So you believe it was Walton who was shot? Why?"

"Bryan, I'm not sure. Ann told me she wanted to get him out of her life. He was shot by the phony Englishman, but I don't think it had to do with the inheritance. It must be related to the Taylor secret in some way. All I know is that's not important right now. What *is* important is that I need the keys to the Land Rover."

"You're going to the Taylor mansion?"

"Yes, Bryan. Mariko is already on her way. See if you can raise Tony and have him join us there as fast as he can."

CHAPTER 39

Let's Get It Over With

They parked the car under the *porte-cochère*. Leaving the unconscious Walton in the car, they got out and surveyed the damage to the estate's grounds.

"Good God! Eli, look—the water is almost to the house!"

"Yeah . . . we don't have long. They will have to close Hillsboro Road soon. You saw the water. It was already spilling across Tyne Boulevard."

"I can't believe that old creek. I never thought about it before. Now it's a white-water river."

"Yeah, babe, it's perfect for us."

"What? What are you going to do, Eli?"

"Ann, we are going to make that pending divorce of yours final. Actually, we're going to turn you into a widow! We are going to float your husband off into the sunset— just another flood victim."

"How? You can't drive over there! The car will bog down in that mud!"

"We don't have to worry about mud. The driveway goes around the big place to the carriage house. Water must be two or three feet high back there, and it's not moving as fast. It only takes about a foot of water to lift a car, especially if we go slowly. All we have to do is start down that driveway, and your car is going to turn into a boat."

"But how do we explain this? I mean, it's *my* car, so why him and not me, or us?"

"That's easy. His motorcycle is still here. As far as anyone knows, he just got here. He saw the two of us together. Everyone knows how jealous he is. He got mad. You had left the keys in your car. He wanted to be a smart-ass and strand us here. Joke was on him. He lost control, and the flood got him."

"Won't the authorities be suspicious if Paul is in the backseat?"

"Hell, after the car is caught by the water and is tossed around a few times, Mr. Walton is going to be all over the place. Look, Ann, we have to do this together. I'll drive. You get in the passenger side. Paul's in the back. Just when the car starts to float, we jump out. You put the battery in your phone and call 911."

All the time Eli had been explaining the plan, Ann was engaged in her own wishful thinking—a different plan. *Yes, Paul arrives to find me with Eli. Paul and Eli fight. Paul could have gotten my gun while at my condo, and he shoots Eli in a jealous rage. He puts Eli in the car. Paul has the gun and forces me to get in also. He tries to drive through high water. I tell him not to. The floodwaters catch my car. I just barely get out, escaping before it is too late. Paul doesn't. Yes, that could be my story. It would be okay that the LadySmith has my prints on it. It's my gun. Paul has handled it, too, so his prints will already be on it.*

"Okay, Ann, let's get it over with."

As they walked back to the car, Ann inserted the battery in her phone, ready to call 911.

CHAPTER 40

Thelma and Louise?

Use of Predator drones on loan from the US military had helped Mark Rollins and his team save lives in previous adventures. Flying a remotely controlled, full-size aircraft over populated civilian areas is frowned upon, however. After Rollins crashed a six-million-dollar Predator into a Belle Meade home, his team started looking for an alternative.

The team purchased six hobby-level operational miniature Predators for one thousand dollars each. They added customized electronics, software, and camera packages that pushed the cost of each of the fifty-two-inch wingspan drones to something between five and six thousand dollars. That was a tiny fraction of the five to ten million dollars that the US government spends on each full-size Predator drone. Of course, the government version can carry armaments and hover over a target for fourteen hours at a maximum height of sixty-five thousand feet. Bryan's drones operated between five and ten thousand feet and have maximum flying time between refueling of three and a half hours.

Bryan was watching the activity on the grounds of the large Taylor estate by way of the bird's-eye view of one of the team's miniatures. The unmanned aerial vehicle was loaded with electronics, including full-motion real-time video for day or night image resolution. In addition to traditional state-of-the-art cameras, the homemade surveillance birds packed infrared and thermal cameras coupled with sophisticated threat detection and image identification software. Bryan had added tunable listening devices, giving their small UAV the ability to pick up audio by bouncing waves off surface areas—glass, plastic, metal, or even wood. That same technology, coupled with powerful software, enhanced 2-D imagery to 3-D–level quality. The multiple images—standard daylight, infrared, and thermal—were each displayed on separate standard-size computer monitors.

Above the three smaller monitors, a software-enhanced composite was displayed on a wall-size monitor in full color. For the composite image, Bryan had the ability to assign colors to image characteristics. For example, water was assigned the color of blue. The deeper the water, the more intense the blue becomes. Green was assigned to terra firma. Structures were assigned transparent shades of white and gray depending on materials. Heat sources displayed as yellow, orange, or red depending on intensity. A joystick provided Bryan with cockpit-like navigational and zoom control.

"Chief, are you at the Taylor place yet?"

"Not yet, Bryan. I had to backtrack. Old Hickory was closed at Granny White. If I don't run into another problem, I should be there in fifteen or twenty minutes."

"Mariko, what about you?"

"I'm still winding my way there, but I will beat the boss."

"Tony, what is your 10-20?"

"Bryan, I love it when you talk police talk. I'm on Hillsboro and about to cross Harding."

"Tony, it's Mariko. I'm just ahead of you."

"Okay guys, listen up. I have three heat images at the Taylor place. Big John just told me they have a match on the Mercedes. And, wait a minute . . . I'll be damned. Sims's phone just went live. We're vectoring in on it, but you can be pretty sure it will point to the Taylor grounds."

"Bryan, this is Mark. Give us a play-by-play."

"At this moment, two images are outside of the car and one remains in the car. The two outside are moving. The car image is stationary, no movement, and I would say the body is in a prone position."

"Can you tell if the image inside the car is dead or alive?"

"It is either alive or was within the last five minutes. It takes about that long for the body temperature to drop. Also, here is another heads-up for you. What was once a creek on the north boundary of the property is now more like a river. Apparently, the low ground is to the west and behind the house. That area appears to be completely flooded to within ten or fifteen feet of the big house. The bad news is that the blue area, the water, is still growing;

and the closer you get to the creek bed, the faster that water is moving."

"Chief, I wish you could see the images coming back from our bird! They are awesome—the surface of water along the creek looks like crumpled paper that is constantly moving. The color is chunky like there is stuff in the water—debris, I'm sure. It's moving *very* fast. The area covered by the overflow has increased just in the last few minutes. From the look of things, the water is going to reach the big house before long. Several out buildings are already flooded."

Mark interrupted, "One of those has to be the large carriage house full of vintage automobiles. The old man never sold anything. The other would have housed the domestics who lived full-time on the premises. It was called the bunkhouse."

"Well, Chief, from the intensity of color, I would say both buildings already have three or four feet of water in them; and, as they say, the creek is still rising. Wait a minute—something is happening. The two images are getting in the car. I'm going to lock onto the car for sound—maybe I can hear what they are saying to each other."

"Bryan, it's Mariko. I'm at the gate. The damn thing is locked."

Rollins asked, "Mariko, can you see the car?"

"Yes, it's starting to move."

"Toward you?"

"No, away. They're driving into the floodwater!"

"What the hell? Are they crazy?—are they doing a Thelma and Louise thing? Mariko, shoot the lock *and hurry*!"

Acting quickly, Mariko got the lock off, swung the gate open, and was re-mounting her bike. Tony blew passed her. "Hey, guys, the cavalry is here. Mariko has the gate open, and I'm moving fast."

Bryan watched the red blotches moving on his computer screen while he began tuning the listening system. He saw Tony and Mariko's red images move toward the darkening blue portion of his computer screen. He watched the transparent image of the car with its three passengers, red engine and exhaust, as it moved from the green portion of the large display monitor to the bright blue area.

After hearing Tony, Rollins pictured the scene in his mind and reacted with a scream. "Tony, stop! Don't ride into the water!"

Tony clamped on the brakes and turned, sliding his bike to a stop just short of the deepening water. Mariko pulled up beside him.

Poole, aka Ann Sims, had the Smith and Wesson in her right hand hidden from Eli's view. She felt the car become light and rock slightly as the water lifted it. That's when Eli shouted, "Time to jump!" It was the last thing he ever said—because that was the same moment she lifted the gun and fired directly into the side of his head.

Mariko and Tony heard the loud report of the .38 followed instantly by Bryan's startled voice. "God, what the hell was that flash? It lit up the entire car, and the sound just about destroyed my ear drums!"

Tony answered, "I think it was a gunshot."

The sound inside the car was deafening and gunpowder burned Ann's eyes. She hadn't expected either. Stunned, it took a few seconds before she could move. They were seconds she didn't have. She threw the gun in the backseat with Paul. There was a sizzling sound. The car's dashboard went dark. The car was moving faster. She tried to open the door. It was locked. She tried to unlock the door. It wouldn't budge. *The window . . . the window . . . I can climb out.* The window controls weren't working. Panic was taking hold of her. *Think, think—stay calm. The gun! Shoot the window. Where is the damn gun?* She couldn't reach it. The car was moving faster. It slammed into a tree. She was thrown forward. Her head smashed against the windshield. Everything dimmed, and then it went black.

Mark Rollins in a black Land Rover pulled up beside Mariko and Tony. The rain had finally stopped. He got out of the car and stood next to his two friends. The three watched along with Bryan from the control room as the car broke free of the tree and began to roll. The car joined other ugly debris, jetsam and flotsam—boiling, crashing, and rolling—pushed by the angry hand of nature.

No one said anything until the car disappeared. Mark said sadly, "Case closed."

"Boss, what the hell happened here?"

"Mariko, I'm not sure we'll ever know exactly. But I have a feeling the world is a better place."

"Mr. R, do you think it had something to do with this old place?"

"I think so, Tony. There's more to what just happened than this old house, but I'm convinced the Taylor mansion holds a secret—a secret that may have been the catalyst to set all this in motion. It's ironic that it ended right where it began."

"Well, Boss, what happens to the place now?"

"You're looking at the new owner. I bought it. With the flood, there was no way the auction was going to take place as scheduled. So my lawyer contacted the judge and the heirs. They accepted my offer. Now, if I have to tear it down to the ground, piece by piece, I'm going to uncover its secret."

CHAPTER 41

Washed Away

We were back at Sperry's for an early dinner. It was Tony, Mariko, Bryan, Sam Littleton, and me. Sperry's had become somewhat of a tradition for us after an adventure ended. We regularly solve problems for WH members. Most of the time, they are pretty insignificant as things go. Certainly, they don't always involve life-and-death issues. Adventures like this one are different. Granted, this time we were never in danger ourselves. Except for shooting the gate lock, we never had to discharge a weapon or even threaten to do so. Nevertheless, people were dead. If we had gotten to the Taylor place even minutes earlier, we might have saved lives. If we had been a little smarter, maybe Eugene Sims would still be alive. You do a lot of second-guessing after something like we just experienced. Our little tradition of getting together at Sperry's is a sort of closure. It's an important step in putting the past behind us. This time we had an additional reason to get together—a little celebration. I had just deposited a check for twenty million dollars—proof that the brain trust was back in full form.

I arrived last and there was a Belvedere martini waiting for me—dry, straight up, and with olives. However, tonight was going to be about wine. I had brought a magnum of *Chateau Cheval Blanc*, vintage 1947. The '47 *Cheval Blanc* has been called the greatest wine on the planet. Wine critic Robert Parker rated the '47 at 100 points—the highest score a wine can receive. This February a single imperial bottle of *Cheval Blanc* '47 sold at Christie's for $304,375.

The five of us completely lost interest in our food as we shared the greatest, most decadent bottle of wine of my life. The single bottle left at the top of the stairs to the secret wine cellar was all that was left of the old mansion. I had the building and its contents demolished and hauled away to join the other debris left behind by Nashville's historic flood event.

But before the demolition, I had discovered the cellar. It was filled almost to the top step of the stairwell with very nasty water. The flood had mixed runoff with raw sewage spilled by city and private processing systems. Runoff from the land had already poisoned floodwater with the remains of animals as well as insecticides and fertilizers. You could smell oil and other chemicals that had mixed with the runoff that had filled our creeks and rivers.

Every bottle of wine in that cellar was more than fifty years old. The corks had become frail and soft, unable to keep out the contaminants. Labels disintegrated and washed away. The glues used in those years were unable to stand up against the tainted water. The flood had washed away a fortune along with the labels.

As we poured the last round of that otherworldly wine, the wine that Mike Steinberger called "a claret from another planet," my iPhone signaled a new text message. I looked down at the screen:

"Mr. Rollins, I have a serious problem and need your help. Please call ASAP—it is critically important!"

Selections from Previous
Mark Rollins Adventures

Chapter 4

Tuesday Morning

It turned cold during the night; at least it was cold for Nashville. The thermometer read 28 degrees outside and a comfortable 71 degrees inside. I was having my every-other-morning breakfast: Cheerios topped with banana slices and a dozen or so raisins with 1% milk plus my usual one cup of coffee per day. Not that the Starbuck's crowd would consider the stuff I drink coffee. Believe it or not, I prefer instant to the real thing.

The breakfast room TV, an LCD, was on Channel 5. I wanted the weather forecast. You have to first pay the price of listening to the anchor recount the overnight home invasions, shootings and convenience store robberies. The bad stuff happens in what the newspeople euphemistically refer to as "South Nashville." Tragically, the description of the victim and the perpetrator usually begins with the words "a black man" or "a Hispanic man."

There was something different this morning. I heard the anchor say "Belle Meade." I heard it too late to get the details of her report. Someone was missing and there was something said about the Women's Health Club. Whatever the story, I needed to know the details. I left the Cheerios to get soggy and moved to my home office. My Dell notebook is always on and connected to the Internet for e-mail so it took only a second to find the story on Channel 5's website:

> *A wealthy Belle Meade businessman is reported missing. Michael Webb, the CEO of New Visions Investments, a Nashville-based private investment bank, disappeared from his Belle Meade home sometime Saturday morning according to his wife, Elizabeth Webb. Mrs. Webb left her home for an appointment with a personal trainer at the Women's Health Club in Brentwood. Michael Webb who collects classic cars was working on a restored Mustang at the time. Mrs. Webb reported that upon her return home around 3:30 p.m., she found a note from her husband. The note indicated that he had some errands to take care of and then a business meeting that would include dinner. He instructed his wife not to wait up for him. When Mrs. Webb awoke Sunday morning to find that her husband was not in the house, she went to the couple's large carriage house that served as a garage and storage area for Mr. Webb's classic car collection.*
>
> *Mr. Webb's Jaguar, the automobile he customarily drives, was parked in its usual place. The Mustang, however, was missing. According to Mrs. Webb, her husband's tools were uncharacteristically scattered around the area. She also observed wipe cloths that*

appeared to be bloody and what she thought
were blood splatters on the floor of the facility.
At that point she called the police.

During a news conference, Chief Carl
Morgan indicated that, at the present time, the
police have no explanation for the disappear-
ance. Chief Morgan said, "Anyone knowing
the whereabouts of Michael Webb or has seen
the missing car should contact the Nashville
Police Department. The car is very distinc-
tive. It is a powder blue 1965 Ford Mustang
convertible in showroom condition with
Tennessee license plate number WEB-07."

In response to questions, Morgan indi-
cated that attempts to reach Michael Webb
via his cell phone had been unsuccessful.

The Channel 5 story gave me a bad feeling. There are
two missing men … a husband and a personal trainer—
our personal trainer. Elizabeth Webb left her husband at
home for an appointment with her personal trainer at *our*
club. Was Rob her trainer? Is there a connection between
Rob's disappearance and the disappearance of Webb? The
thought was disturbing.

I gave Sarah a kiss and headed for Black Beauty and
a quick trip to the WH Club. Black Beauty is my slick
Lexus LS sedan with all the bells and whistles and a few
non-standard ones added by my IT brain trust. Some of
the stuff would make 007 proud.

Fifteen minutes later I pulled into the back lot of the
WH Club. It was 6:15 in the morning but there were al-

ready 15 or 20 Jags, BMWs, and Mercedes in the lot. I spotted Meg's copper colored Mini Cooper in its usual spot. Meg is who I wanted to see this morning—and the sooner the better.

Chapter 6

Ramiro Melendez

Ramiro Melendez was in the US illegally, but he was hardly welcome in his own country. He was on the run from Mexican authorities after jumping bail. His rap sheet starts at age nine when the local grocer had him arrested for shoplifting. But it was his latest predicament that sent him to the US. He killed a man. As Ramiro saw it, the guy had it coming to him, and it had been a fair fight—but he had been the brother of a member of the State Chamber of Deputies.

Ramiro's attorney was an American lawyer. Ramiro wasn't stupid; he reasoned that an American lawyer living in Mexico and working in a "nothing" Mexican law firm meant that his lawyer probably couldn't live or practice law in the US. He was right. After his lawyer managed to get him out of jail on bail by bribing a local judge, Ramiro and his lawyer worked out a deal.

The Melendez family was not poor. Ramiro didn't steal out of need. Stealing was easier than working. Lying was easier than honesty. When Ramiro wanted something, he wanted it immediately. The idea of working hard and saving for things never entered his mind. Ramiro was a long-time problem for the Melendez family so when he asked for money to leave the country, they were only too happy to contribute. Most of the hundred thousand pesos went to Ramiro's lawyer. The lawyer supplied him with documents—a US birth certificate, Social Security number, and a Tennessee driver's license. Except for the birth certificate, the documents were not forged; they were authentic. Ramiro's lawyer had connections in Tennessee. Even in the US, you can find underpaid government employees willing to do things for a little extra money. Tennessee drivers' licenses—genuine licenses—are for sale if you know the right employee. Ramiro didn't know which one, but his lawyer told him that someone who worked in a Memphis Driver's License branch would issue a license to anyone for $500. You send them $500, a name, address, and photograph, and they will deliver the license with no questions asked. There was one other part of the deal. Ramiro was to check in with his lawyer monthly. Why? As the lawyer explained, there might come a time when Ramiro could do the lawyer a favor—one that would put money in both their pockets.

Ramiro Melendez found his way to Tennessee and eventually blended into the predominantly Hispanic Nashville community, Antioch. He worked part-time on different landscaping crews but only long enough to identify targets for his more lucrative craft. He was a good thief and his hunting grounds were always in upscale neighborhoods. He picked easy targets. Power tools, chainsaws, and bicycles from unsecure garages provided spending money. The *real* money was in jewelry and watches stolen from unlocked homes while the husband was away at work and the wife was working in their flowerbeds or gardens.

Ramiro wasn't stupid; but his victims were. He got a good laugh when he thought about it. Their homes always had signs posted warning about their security systems, but the alarms were never turned on during the day. That is when he did his work. He stayed away from night work or homes where the people appeared to be away on trips or vacation. That is when alarms were set. He picked houses where the lady was working in her garden. Those were easy and quick. He would slip into the house and find the master bedroom. There was always a jewelry box. He would grab the most expensive looking things and get the hell out *pronto*! He never spent more than five or ten minutes doing a job. He was long gone before the robbery was ever discovered. He liked it even better when there were landscaping people working on the grounds. He could walk right into the house without anyone noticing. If there should be someone inside the house, he would go into his "*agua* routine." He would become a poor hard-working Mexican looking for water—who apologetically doesn't speak the language. They would quickly send him out of the house, but no one ever called the cops. It always worked. They were stupid; he wasn't.

Ramiro watched the local news because he wanted to see if the newspeople ever talked about his robberies. They never did. But he *did learn* why his lawyer was in Mexico. The woman the lawyer had been living with had disappeared. People think she is dead—and they think the lawyer did it—but they haven't found her body. The unsolved case continues to be talked about on the evening news. The police want to question the lawyer but can't get to him in Mexico. The missing woman's parents are keeping the case alive. They say they want justice. Ramiro thinks they want revenge, and he thinks there might be some money opportunities for him. He decides to find out where the woman's parents live. He may want to have a discussion with them at some point.

Chapter 6

"Ding Dong"

"Mr. Nelson, I just learned about Lansden!" shouted Gordon Seemann.

"Yeah, the "great litigator" is dead. Makes you want to sing, doesn't it?" The man laughed and began chanting, "Ding Dong! The old barrister is dead. Which old barrister? The Wicked Barrister! Ding Dong! The Wicked Barrister is dead." At the end of his out-of-tune ditty, he asked, "Has a nice ring to it, doesn't it?"

"Mr. Nelson, the man is dead! Aren't we being a little too flippant about it?" Seemann wondered if Nelson had gone over the edge.

Keith Nelson was fifty-eight. He was a big man, seated behind a big desk in a big office. He had worked on Wall Street most of his life. Million dollar bonuses had been amassed into an even bigger fortune. He needed that fortune to support his lifestyle. Now, with a new wife and just when he was beginning to enjoy that wealth, it was all at risk—at risk because of that stubborn-ass country lawyer, Lansden, out to make a name for himself.

When the housing boom really started taking off, Nelson was smart enough to see the mortgage refinancing opportunity. With interest rates on the decline and home values skyrocketing, the new generation of homeowners had discovered they could turn their homes into an ATM machine. They could get ready cash to pay down credit cards or other bills just by refinancing. So what if that meant higher mortgage payments? They could just run up the credit cards again and in a couple of years do another refi. Nelson saw that he could pocket big fees by handling the paperwork and passing the risk on to others.

He left the investment firm and started his own mortgage company, Hudson Bluff Mortgage, Inc. The system was rigged, and he saw that it was a game you could not lose. He used to say, "I don't take the risk, just the profits." Get him talking, and he would let you know how it is done. "You close a refi deal. You sell that paper to some dumb-as-hell bureaucrat. You take that money and make more deals. You just do it over and over again. That is all we do—turn the money and take the profits. The bureaucrats bundle the mortgages into $100 million packages that the people on Wall Street are all too happy to sell—for a fee—to institutional and fund investors all over the world. Then the money flows back into the mortgage refi market. It is just one big recycling of money. Everyone is happy. Everyone is making money." . . . "That was until the shit hit the fan," he later said.

"Gordon, you don't understand! You should be celebrating. Your butt has just been pulled out of the fire. That bastard, Lansden, had us by the balls over the Fenio mortgage case. Hell, Fenio hocked his house to start a bunch of taco stands—refinanced their place for a hell of a lot more than it was worth. He didn't even have a job. Lost his shirt—and, when the bank was foreclosing, Fenio's wife goes running to the Great Harold T. Lansden claiming we shouldn't have loaned the damn money! We are supposed to have told Fenio it was okay to lie like shit on the application. Lansden was going to sue us for the big bucks!

To hell with the money—after he got through with the two of us, I figured we would be damn lucky to stay out of jail. Hell, we were both going to be ruined by that hillbilly. I'm the CEO; you're the CFO. We are the people the public wants to see swinging from a lamppost. We are the "corporate fat cats." Obama, that damn Congress, and the fucking news media has whipped our dumb-as-a-post citizens into a pitchfork marching mob. This time they aren't after Frankenstein—they want a piece of *you* and *me*. They want to stick those pitchforks into some mean, bad corporate executives!"

Gordon Seemann was a young CPA. He joined the staff of a large national CPA firm right out of college. Three years later, he was the senior member of the audit team assigned to the Hudson Bluff Mortgage, Inc. account. It was Seemann's job to review the accounting firm's proposed management letter with Mr. Nelson before issuing the final report to the Board of Directors. The initial draft had been strongly critical of a number of practices followed by the company. Mr. Nelson got the young CPA to drop some and soften other recommendations. Two months after completion of the audit, Gordon Seemann joined the mortgage company as its Chief Financial Officer.

"Mr. Nelson, I don't understand what we are supposed to have done that was so bad. We have 6,000 employees and 4,000 agents and independents. We can't know what every one of those is doing all the time. How can they make us responsible for a few over enthusiastic sales types who went overboard?"

"Gordon, we are the worst kind of bad guys—fat cats with big salaries. Lansden would have convinced the jury that we deliberately set out to rip off old people, widows, and orphans. You and I know it wasn't that way. Right? Everyone was supposed to be working off the same forms. Everyone was using "stated income" so we could commit on the spot. If we hadn't gone along with it, we wouldn't have had any business. The competition didn't give us time to verify the income information. Like everybody else—we let the applicants fill in their income information on the application form. We take their word for it. The applicants swear to it. What are we supposed to do, call our customers liars and crooks?

We had some bad apples like everyone else. Our jerk agent in that hick-town Nashville was one of them. Okay, so he told people what to put on the forms. They say he recruited refis—showed people how they could get some real spending money by borrowing more than their house was worth. Damn fools took the money and blew it—big ass vacations, gambling, or whatever. Hell, they just pissed it away! Then the buffoons could not afford the damn payments. And, that is supposed be *our* fault? How were we supposed to know that? Hell, we were, what, 1500 miles away in New York? We gave them the damn book. We told them to follow the damn thing. What the hell did they think we wrote those procedures for? We depend on people to follow our rules, right? If they don't, if they do bad things, then *they* are the jerks who should be hauled to court—sent to jail. Not us!"

"Mr. Nelson, Nashville wasn't the only place. A lot of that stuff was going on in Orange County, right? So why is Nashville such a big problem?"

"Gordon, the problem wasn't about Nashville. It was about that dead bastard, Lansden. He wasn't just some lawyer. He was a damn politician. That guy was trying to make a national name for himself. Hell, the man actually thought he could be the *President*. We are taking care of those Orange County problems. We're doing it quietly. That damn Lansden wasn't into doing things quietly. Nashville could have snowballed and taken us down. Lansden wanted blood—ours!

It is different now. The "great litigator" is dead—no more gravy train for the other partners in his law firm. Lansden's firm is going to have their hands full trying to fill his shoes. Hell, they can't do it! H.T. Lansden was a busy man—had a zillion balls in the air. With Lansden out of the picture, we can head this thing off before it does snowball, or worse, lead to a class action suit. We need to get to the client and settle—and get them to sign a non-disclosure agreement. We make them an offer they can't refuse, but one we can afford."

"I wish I shared your optimism, Mr. Nelson. The law firm may not roll over on this. What if they want to hold out for a mega jury verdict?"

"They don't have any reason to go big time with this. It was Lansden's ambition that was driving this. They are smarter than that. They know how long a court case would take. We would appeal. If we slow-walked things, it would be years before the client or the law firm would see one damn penny. Hell, the publicity would destroy us anyway, and their jury award would be worthless. Lansden didn't give a shit about the money. A settlement will immediately put money in the firm's bank account. It will be one less of Lansden's hot potatoes that the firm has to deal with. And Lansden's death may have them worrying about their own hides. The timing is right. It always pays to take advantage of someone else's misery."

"Anything I can do to help, Mr. Nelson?"

"Gordon, it wouldn't hurt to have a friend inside Lansden's law firm—someone who keeps us posted—maybe even in a position to encourage the Fenios to accept the settlement."

"We may have an inside man—someone we have been cultivating, just in case. He contacted us about a job—a big salary position in our legal department, Assistant General Counsel. He hinted that he might be able to help us out with the Fenio case. I've been stringing him along."

"Who is it?"

"His name is Bill Maxwell."

"How far down the ladder is he?"

"He claims he is one of three senior associates they have talked to about moving to partner level."

Nelson expressed his skepticism, "Wouldn't that kind of make our job less attractive to him?"

"The firm has a funny compensation system. I won't bore you with the details, but according to Maxwell the only thing being a partner gets you in that firm is personal liability for the firm's debt and for malpractice claims."

"See what you can get out of him. Who is going to take over the Fenio case? Is there any chance he can get involved through his end—help us get this thing settled

ASAP? You can tell him it would make the Assistant General Counsel job his. Hell, tell him it will be Vice President and Assistant General Counsel."

"Will do."

"Yep, Gordon, you should celebrate. It is a good day. The Wicked Barrister is dead, or maybe I should say the Bastard is dead—and good riddance to him!"

"Mr. Nelson, you seem a little too happy about this."

"You bet your ass, I'm happy!"

"I mean, we didn't have anything to do with this, did we?"

Keith Nelson laughed. "Why Gordon, how can you ask such a thing? I'm just the Good Bastard whose house fell on the Bad Bastard. It was an act of God." He looked up at the ceiling, raised his hands, and laughed as he exclaimed, "Thank you, God!"

Then Nelson stopped laughing and focused on Seemann. "And you should thank God too, Gordon. If Lansden had had his way, your stock options would be worthless. You would be out of a job—*penniless*. The only job you could get is as a shoe salesman, or worse, a mattress salesman. Jail might have even looked good to you— a roof over your head and three squares a day. Count your blessings, my son, and don't question good fortune when it comes your way. Just keep thinking—Ding Dong! The Wicked Barrister is dead!"

ABOUT TOM COLLINS
AUTHOR, ENTREPRENEUR, AND EPICUREAN

 The London-based publication *Citytech* called him an "outstanding individual and visionary" when M. Thomas (Tom) Collins was named as one of the Top 100 Global Tech Leaders in the legal community. Tom Collins, as he prefers to be called, is also the recipient of the Lifetime Achievement Award from the US Publication *Law Technology News* for his contribution to the use of technology in the legal community. Although now retired from the commercial world, he continues to write and speak on the subject of management and pen his Mark Rollins adventure series of mysteries.

www.I65North.com

Tom Collins is available for selected readings and lectures. To inquire about a possible appearance, contact PLA Media at 615-327-0100 or info@plamedia.com. To contact the author, e-mail tom.collins@markrollinsadventures.com.

CPSIA information can be obtained at www.ICGtesting.com
Printed in the USA
LVOW06*1021270713

344906LV00001B/2/P